THE ROUTE

P J Walters

Waggledance Press

In memory of
J S B Walters
'King of the Road Number'

HOME

I don't know whether it's the rain, but it's darker inside than I remember. It's also quieter. All I can hear are the raindrops pattering on the corrugated roof far above.

I have left the seat of the van for the last time. The engine is ticking with the raindrops as it goes cold.

I loiter outside the big shutter door. It is half open. Why? Have they had a delivery or are they waiting for me to deliver myself?

I can't hear them inside. Stranger still, I can't hear the sound of the video. Yet they must be inside, because their cars are parked by the wall.

I stay at the door, looking into the quiet shade. Nothing is moving. I think of the knight-errant at the mouth of the cave, ready to face the fate beast, and I try to see myself from the outside. I can't. There is no music, no fancy camera work, no glorious Technicolor on this drab day.

I feel stupid, because I'm going to stop putting off going in because I'm getting damp, and not for any of the other reasons. So in I go...

M25

Not for the first time the clockwise carriageway of the M25 had come to a standstill. So had I, right in the thick of it in my white Astra van, staring at the lines of traffic extending endlessly into the December drizzle. I'd really wanted this last trip to go smoothly, but there I was – another stationary tin box on the northern curve of the great doughnut. 10:25 AM. I'd been gone from the unit nearly an hour and I still hadn't passed Rickmansworth.

I turned off my wipers and let the drizzle accumulate on the windscreen. Dots became smears became rivulets became deltas sliding down the glass. The outside world blurred and I sat alone with my load, trying as hard as I could not to think.

This time there were thirty boxes in the back – thirty boxes about the size of a wine case, forming two even layers on the load floor. I looked back to see if they were still there, as if anything could have happened to them without me noticing. They looked back at me, as inscrutable as ever, yet they had caused me all this trouble. Three years ago there wouldn't have been more than a dozen, which just goes to show how much business has grown.

The mass of vehicles moved forward a car length. I

switched the wipers on for two sweeps and turned them off again. It's at times like these that I wish the entire surface of the motorway was able to rotate on some giant mechanism at say, ten miles an hour. Then we could all lie back and relax until it was time to shuffle off to our appropriate exits. It would be like a sleepy carrousel. Instead you have to put up with the clutch-balancing-crawl: an insult to forward momentum and excessively taxing for the clutch leg.

It's strange to have seen Gail again after all this time. Stranger still to have heard her voice. You can't always remember quite how some things are. They get distorted somehow, like traffic through the rain-soaked window. Actively ignoring them adds to the distortion so, when you do get uninvited flashbacks, they're even less like anything to do with reality.

'Oi, you dozy cunt, shift it.'

I brought myself back to the gap that had opened up in front of me. Such a thing cannot be countenanced in the push and shove of the world's largest gar park. So I made up the distance in about three seconds and we were all back where we started. Fuckwit behind was leaning out of his window, trying to transfix my reflection in the driver's mirror. I wound down the window and stared back until his resolve broke. I would rather have broken his back, but you can't really do that sort of thing. At least not without an escape route.

Shame it had to be raining. Last time I got this stuck it was a lovely summer's day. Can't remember which summer, but I do remember it was caused by a wagon shedding its load of gas cylinders across all three carriageways this side of Chorley Wood. The word got passed down the line: no one was going anywhere for a long time.

People got out of their cars and stood around. Everyone turned off their engines. I stood on the motorway. I had never actually stood on a motorway. Now there were hundreds of us standing out in the sunshine. Some were bitching about the state of the road network; others were having a joke about it. There were people who would normally be up each other's tail pipes having a laugh in light-hearted resignation to the facts. I walked up the carriageway. A group of people was sharing a flask of tea, a clutch of sales reps were playing one-upmanship with their vehicle specs, a flamenco troupe was practising a routine on the hard shoulder. Further on an ice-cream van had opened up shop and was doing major trade. It was like a holiday.

I wandered on, past an empty white van not unlike mine, transmitting the unmistakable sounds of sexual congress from its dark interior. The car in front of the van was empty. I could see a lipstick lying on the driver's seat and I knew, I just knew, that she was back there with the van driver and that this was the first time they had met. Such was the magic of the sunny day and the columns of traffic on the no-go-road.

Back to the drizzle and another car length crawl to add to the total of elapsed miles. My windscreen was misting up, as if the mist was blowing directly through the vents and depositing itself on the inside of the glass. I turned the heater up full and wound down the passenger window for the through draught. The engine of an ancient Luton rattled in my ear, a sonorous chatter telling me that its little ends were on the way out. I was on my own way out. In three days I would be back and everything would become clear. Again I looked over my shoulder and glanced at the load, as if the glancing could make it any more secure or outcomes any different.

I once took thirty-one boxes: not a good number. However I tried I couldn't get the last box to wedge in with the two perfect layers made up by the other thirty. It ended up sitting by itself on top, just inside the back doors. Inelegant loading smacks of amateurism. It smacks of something else, too. Three roundabouts out from the unit the fool in front of me pulled to a halt even though there wasn't another vehicle in sight. I was busy checking right, ready to sail straight across. It came as something of a shock, then, when I returned my attention to the forward direction, to see a fat Jag blocking my path. I stamped on my brakes and avoided his bumper by the thickness of a fag paper. Needless to say, he chose that moment to carry on, oblivious of the near miss. Box thirty-one, on its smooth, unbroken run of fellow boxes, traversed the entire length of the van and twatted me on the back of the head. All the van's forward momentum must have must have been transferred into that one box, because it cricked my neck in a way that lingered for weeks. When I got to Dawn's house, regardless of my best intentions, I even had to cry off our usual activities which, as it had been all of six weeks since the last time, didn't go down at all well. The box spent the rest of its journey in the passenger foot well and it was first out at the first drop.

The Luton rattled on and I looked up for a break in the clouds. Anything other than drizzle, preferably a light dusting of snow and clear skies. The damp keeps the fumes down amongst the cars. The clutch-balancing-crawl makes lots of fumes, with its simultaneous rushing-forward and grinding-to-a-halt, puffing out clouds of coal-black diesel particulates. Human beings aren't designed to breathe that sort of shit.

Now it was getting beyond a joke. I was really going to struggle to make up time. One of the drops was time dependent. Not just that, but being late is not professional. I like to be professional. On my last trip I want to be the epitome of professionalism. The rain was coming in my window and my breath was forming fumes, like an exhaust. My stomach was burning. If we didn't get a move on soon I would be breathing fire. I turned on the radio to try and take my mind off it and, as if by magic, it was Gigi with the traffic report.

"Well, I think I can kill two birds with one stone here, Colin. The reason I'm in two hours early is because Alice has rung in to say that she has been unavoidably detained by heavy traffic on the A41. Traffic is moving slowly, but it's also causing a tail back onto the M25 at

Junction 19, causing major delays for drivers on the clockwise carriageway…"

No shit.

"…which is why you have the dubious pleasure of my company this morning."

"So, Traffic Alice is caught in traffic."

"Er, yes. In fact, I have the green light to go all the way through to my usual slot in this afternoon if she doesn't make it, although Badger Bill has rung in from his lorry. He's further into town on the same route and he thinks the blockage is just about to be cleared, so we might see her yet."

"Well, thank you Gigi, we'll expect you then for the normal report just before eleven."

"That's it."

Sometimes Gigi's reports contain a spell. No sooner had she finished telling me that it was going to get easier than the traffic started to ease up. I got into second gear for a while, then third. Come on Gigi, cast your magic over the entire trip. Make it go easy. Up into fourth feeling that acrid pain in my stomach. Best put it down to the caustic bile that serves as coffee back at the unit. I changed up to fifth, reached into the glove box for my packed lunch and, purely for antacid purposes, ate it for breakfast.

DAVENTRY

'When are you coming back then, John?' Dawn asked me when we last met.

'No way of knowing,' I said. 'It's down to the order book and orders from the boss. A couple of months, maybe. There was such a lot last time I shouldn't think anyone will need to restock until after Christmas.'

That was just to give me some leeway. The trips had been getting more regular. Either the customers were selling more or they had some reason for building up the reserves. Either way, I didn't know about it.

'We could have a bottle. They wouldn't miss a-one, would they?'

'Dawn, there's twelve bottles in a case. Say they're having five cases, that's sixty bottles. They can count the difference between sixty and fifty-nine. It's all first growth stuff and it's worth a mint, there's no way we'd get away with knocking one back ourselves. If you want a bottle of wine we'll go to the offy and I'll buy you one, whatever you want.'

'The stuff they have at the offy is shit, I want some of the good stuff you've got in the van. One of these days I'm going to wait until you're asleep and get the keys to the van and help myself.'

'You really, really don't want to do that.'

I hoped she would hear the serious note in my otherwise jocular tone. She couldn't know that it wasn't wine, in the same way that she couldn't know that my name wasn't John.

'All right, but you've got to promise me you'll bring some for us next time.'

'It's fucking fifty quid a bottle stuff.'

'You must get a staff discount or something. There's got to be some perk to you coming and going all the fucking time.'

'I'm a perk in myself,' I said and took a bow.

'You're a big-headed bastard and you're full of shit. You should piss off rather than bothering me all the time.'

She had a point, even if she was half-joking herself. I could see she was pleased as hell to see me. Another time I might bring her something special in the wine department, but there was no way I was going to let her get her hands on the keys to the van.

That was last time. I was going again and it had been barely a month. In that month I had learned more than I really wanted to know, but still didn't know what I needed to know. I'd know soon enough. Part of me wanted to explain to Dawn, but how can you explain that sort of stuff? I couldn't even explain it to myself.

I turned onto the northern dart of the M1 – the point where I always think the journey 'proper' starts. The

M25 is a circle: as soon as you start you are coming back. My delivery route is a cycle in itself, but when you're sat facing north at the beginning of this road, shown as a great blue vein on the map, you feel like you can keep on driving forever.

I was hemmed in amongst a mass of wagons come in that day via the southern ports. Sometimes going north is like starting off uphill. I was still running late. Time was I could have taken the A5 and taken my time, but the schedule didn't allow for that anymore, not with the Yorkshire rendezvous. On the A5 you can kid yourself you're following in the footsteps of Romans, not the clogged arteries of modernist ambition: the M1 is only slightly older than myself.

I was stuck amongst all those churning wagons, trying to make up time, at the same time not wanting to reach the first drop too soon. I don't like those people there. *Never let a smile pollute your face* – that's their motto. I didn't feel much like smiling myself, but thinking about Dawn might make it happen. Perhaps not, not when I think about the things I'm going to have to do to sort that one out. The half-formed smile drops from my face.

I found myself in a small pocket of calm, a hundred yards of clear space between the traffic in front and the traffic behind. Such oases are getting rarer nowadays and are to be savoured while you can – the eye of the storm is disappointingly finite.

I looked at the dash clock: later still. Maybe later I could break the rules and speed a little. Maybe later I would have to.

Herts. became Beds., now further in body and mind from all the ramifications of the unit. Much better – even with the twat in the green Renault flashing me from behind. I jabbed my brakes to make him think. He'd be annoyed, but what did I care?

'You wanna do acid?' Dawn said to me.

'Why should I want to do that?'

'You know, to get high.'

'And acid will do that, will it?'

'Yeah, you know, takes you away to a better place, away from all this shit.'

'I might like all this shit.'

'But you always look so unhappy.'

'Do I?' Of course I had no idea, I didn't look at myself in the mirror these days. I didn't have a mirror in my place.

'Don't you like getting off your face?'

There were too many connotations involved in that question. She wanted a simple answer, but I wasn't going to give her one, 'Depends what you mean?'

'You know, seeing the other side of stuff?'

'What other side?'

'You're not going to tell me you've never dropped a tab?'

'Well yes, I have.'

'What, recently?'

'No, not for a while.'

'Then you've forgotten what it's like.'

'It's precisely because I haven't forgotten what it's like that I'm not going to take it again now.'

'What do you mean?'

'Dawn, I'm pretty sure you can take the stuff and not have to worry too much about what's in store. I'm not so sure I can do that.'

'You're scared.'

'I'm not scared of the acid, I just don't want to go to the places it's likely to take me.'

'What are you on about?'

'How shall I put this? Look, sometimes when you're driving about and you're not on some schedule you might decide to take a left when you had planned for a right, just because it looks interesting that way, yeah?'

'Do you?'

'Just take it from me, as someone who's done a lot of turning left and right, that that's the sort of thing you do.'

'All right.'

'Well sometimes you see something that makes the detour worthwhile. Most of the time though, you don't, it's a waste of time and you wish you'd stuck to your route.'

'So?'

'Often the road less travelled is less travelled for a reason. I mean, why bother to go all the way to John O'Groats when every time you've been it's been shrouded in fog?'

'But I got us a couple of tabs.'

'Really, I'm fine. I'll drink these couple of beers. If you want to take one be my guest, I'll make sure everything's okay.'

'Okay for what?'

'I'll keep an eye on you while you're tripping.'

She looked at me as if she didn't understand or, rather, that I didn't understand something. Then she took both tabs.

I watched her all evening and through to the early hours. When the neighbours phoned I turned the music down. I drank my few bottles of beer and watched her dance. I watched her staring at the picture on a CD case. I listened to her extended thesis on 'purpular sound'. I enjoyed the quiet when she sat on the settee for two hours smiling into space. I let myself feel superior in my sanity and reserve, then realised that what I was feeling was envy. How could someone let themselves go to that degree, to get right to the end of themselves and find nothing ill, or split or spilled? What had happened to me on the way?

The next day she was up and bright and making breakfast and I felt like a hungover dog.

'Bet you wished you'd dropped one,' she said.

'Just be glad I didn't,' I replied.

Steady going at sixty-five miles an hour. Fewer people butting in and out of the slip roads. Late morning, the lower number junctions left behind. Still not on time.

The first time I went to Daventry it was a hell of a job

to find the drop. I had been told it was one of the units on the industrial estate. Fair enough, but there are uncountable, indistinguishable industrial estates from which to select. They're like the moons of Saturn, dotted around the planetary ring road. I ended up pissing around for over an hour and finding myself twice going back out on the A45. I felt like one of those who, trying to escape the desert, find that they've spent three days walking in a giant circle and are now out of water. The next time I invested in a street plan and went straight to the place. Lesson? Always have a plan.

The dash clock said eleven forty-five, but at least I was there. They were there to meet me.

I had never been inside the unit. Whatever the weather its doors were open, even with sleet cutting onto the floor. Whatever the quality of light it always looked dark inside. Sparks flew in the darkness and machine noise echoed in the void. They did something like reline brake shoes or clutch plates. No one ever volunteered any information and there was no factory sign to elucidate. It looked like a foul place to work. The employees were denizens of the underworld and wrought swords and axe-heads for their dread lord, Vulcan.

I called them 'the twins'. They were almost exactly alike, except that one was black and one was white. Both were bald, in their late twenties at most. Both were gymnasium monsters. They looked to me as if they did unspeakable things to animals in their spare time.

'You're fucking late,' one of them said.

'Traffic,' I said

'Oh yeah? Let's get the fuckers off.'

I opened the back of the van while they wheeled up a trolley. Sooner gone the better. I handed over a box.

'Careful, careful,' said black twin, 'we don't want any fucking accidents.'

His big hands held on to the box, not taking it off me, holding it in to my chest so that he and it remained in my personal space.

'If you want,' I said. You could have dropped a box from six feet – the stuff was packaged to survive. Still, there was no point telling him that: precious meant fragile. The stuff was precious because it was expensive. Because it was expensive it was fragile.

He took the box off me, then another three. Each time he made sure we were both holding on to the box for longer than was strictly necessary to hand it over. I went along with it. When there were four on the trolley white twin took it away. Black twin kept his eyes on me all the time, as if I might do something that required remedial action. He was willing that thing to happen. There was no way he was going to take his eyes off me until I had left the premises. For that reason alone I took my time locking the back, getting in, securing my seatbelt, adjusting the rear-view mirror, adjusting the door mirror, starting up and driving off.

DESPATCH

I don't know why I'd been so bothered about the hell twins. It wasn't as if I'd have to see them again. I didn't have to see Daventry again. Oh the joy.

There was no point trying to rush. A whole new swathe of traffic had caught up while I'd been at the drop. Traffic is inexhaustible. You wonder where it all comes from, what all these thousands of individuals can be up to. People have to *be* places, it seems. Create an idea, say the internal combustion engine, and all its possibilities have to be explored up to and beyond the logical conclusion. Build a new road and traffic appears from nowhere to fill it. The M1 was supposed to be the new, clear highway to the North, a fast-track road with no speed limits. On this wet day it's a constant shunt between the gears, watching time evaporate on the dash clock.

The Leicester junction came and went. Leicester Forest East: I couldn't see a single tree. Coalville, Loughborough, Donington. How did I get here? How did I get to this state of consequences?

A steel wagon joined from the slip road. I was once on the M18, travelling in light traffic. There was a pickup going steady on the inside lane. I caught up and passed. There was something wrong. As it went along, steel reinforcing grids, the type you lay in wet concrete, were dropping off the back. I pulled alongside and tried to get the driver's attention, but he was on a planet far away from the risk he was creating. I had no phone; I was miles away from the nearest payphone. On the road behind the grids were bouncing to a halt, directly in the path of oncoming vehicles. How could someone be so shit-brained not to secure their load, and then not to notice when it was bouncing off the back? Those things must weigh a couple of hundredweight apiece.

I never got to a phone. For some stupid reason, by the time I got on the A1 and the possibility of contacting the Police, my own journey had taken precedence. I left it. Yet if a motorcycle had hit one of those grids...

I am a biker – that's how I know the risks. Not that I ride full-time anymore. I had to sell my old bike. It paid a month's rent and a couple of bills that had gone dark red. It put off nothing: I still ended up having to leave my flat.

Consequences. You forget how awkward it is to go about getting buses and arranging trains, how have to forget about just 'popping' over somewhere. The practical difficulties of simply getting to a place often outweigh the advantages. So, as soon as my transport was gone, I was looking for a way to get some more, because sometimes, on a whim, you need to be somewhere else.

I rode despatch. In fact, I rode despatch in London.

Central London, Greater London, all over fucking London.

There were half a dozen of us on the day shift – the shift that included both the morning and evening rush hours and the lunchtime melee. All the busiest hours of the day we were out there, negotiating the traffic, trying to avoid the pitfalls, getting 'performance motivation' via the headset.

'Benny, where the fuck are you? That was a fifteen-minute drop. You've been on it half an hour. Get your fucking finger out. I'd have done three by now. Get over to Dimitri's toot sweet...roger? Oi, are you listening?'

'Roger that Base, stuck in traffic, Bayswater. Current drop ETA three minutes, Dimitri's ten plus, out.'

'Halle-fuckin'-lujah, advise after collection...Benny?...Benny?...fuck it...Benny?'

'Roger Base...at drop now...will advise, out.'

I hated them calling me Benny. It's the sort of name you give a cuddly toy. I'm Benjamin or Ben if you want. The dispatchers always called me Benny over the air. I suppose it was like calling a dog back – a two-syllable name works the best... 'Toby, Toby, here boy.'

There was always a disparity between what they expected and what could be achieved. None of the despatch team were riders themselves: they were employed purely for their articulacy. The dispatchers promised the customer an unfeasible collection and delivery schedule and then sent us, the shock troops, to provide the service. Trying to keep to the schedule was the next best thing to suicide.

Two things happen. First, you are invisible to almost all traffic. A quarter of a ton of bike and rider, the former with lights lit regardless of time of day, the latter wearing a fluorescent tabard over his leather body armour, transmute into a two-dimensional shape which the average car driver can only see the split second after he has slammed you into a row of ornate iron railings bordering the Queen's highway. Secondly, you are a black hole for all the hurt and anguish in the known universe. We all know that city driving is a frustrating, time-consuming, bumper-to-bumper lesson in the futility of existence, but it must be borne with humour and good grace. When you see the nimble despatch rider, on his agile steed, skilfully threading his way through available gaps in the gridlock, he is not the sly bastard who fucked your girlfriend while you were watching satellite football with your mates in the William IV. Neither is he responsible for the shed load of pasta sauce, which is at this very moment turning the Marble Arch roundabout into a pizza base. The rider too has a job to do and must use whatever opportunities present themselves within the boundary of the law. Therefore, he is not to be glared at, beeped at, sworn at, punched at, to have doors opened in his path, to have egress denied by a spiteful turn of the steering wheel, to be blocked in at box junctions in contravention of the Highway Code or to be treated as a mirage when entering a roundabout. The rider is largely unprotected and appreciates the consideration of all road users. He has little choice to respect them, because they are mostly heavy and hard.

'Benny, Benny, where are you? Dimitri's been on the blower, says he's going over to cycle despatch if you're not there in five, says it can't be any fuckin' slower than this. Benny, you reading? Where are you?'

'Roger that Base. Currently in shop doorway, Edgware road, ETA unobtainable.'

'Benny, Benny, what do you mean?'

'Some cunt in a minicab knocked me off the bike…bike riding me in doorway…will advise…out.'

That was riding. It was hectic, pressured, tiring, but it had its compensations: the pay was okay, the bike got serviced regularly, and there was a certain camaraderie amongst the riders.

Employee turnover was fairly high, partly because of the pressure and partly because of injuries. If you stuck it out long enough you could acquire the skills, but most people didn't get through the first few weeks of shell shock. Those who did were usually okay to be around. I suppose that's always the case with high-risk occupations. It was only motorcycle delivery, but you went out there every day with the knowledge that you could find yourself spread thinly down the side of a wagon heading east with a load of halal goat.

Some of the boys took the odd substance to keep themselves sharp; they were the ones who usually got the sharp end. I always thought I'd be better calm and crystal clear. In reality I must have been hopped up on adrenaline, because the strain was telling on me without me seeing it build up. It was only a matter of time.

It was a typical incident. I was at the head of a queue, on the inside of two lanes, just in front of a van, coming up to a pelican crossing with the green turning to amber. Another van was overtaking the one behind. He started to pull in, to the left. I knew he hadn't seen me because he was driving blind... and deaf, because even when I sounded my horn he kept on coming across. There were railings to my left – nowhere to go. He was going to run me up the wall. The only thing to do was accelerate ahead and hope the bike was quick enough. The green man can't have been up, because the light had still not gone to red. Nevertheless, there was someone in a grey suit starting to cross, a man in a grey suit with a green spotted tie talking into a mobile and eating a grilled vegetable sandwich, heavy on the peppers. I know this because in the instant I swerved past him I saw it all. I was so close I could almost hear what he was saying.

By then I was travelling too fast. I shot over the crossing and onto the roundabout beyond. The bike formed itself into an elongated 'S' shape and found its way between two black cabs and an old, pagoda Mercedes before pitching onto the grass of the island and coming to an abrupt halt.

'Base, this is Ben, advise, please send another rider to pick-up, unable to proceed.'

'No can do Benny, proceed to pick-up, fuckin' pronto, customer waiting.'

After that I made my way up to the M40 and let her rip for a stretch, just to clear my head. By the time I got back I was out of a job. Not long after that I sold the bike to pay the rent. One small event leads to bigger things.

M1

I like driving. It's a kind of dream. Sure, you're concentrating all the way, making sure you do the right thing in any given situation, but at the same time it's unreal. People were designed to walk. When you're walking things come up and pass slowly, giving you plenty of time to take them in. By the time you'd walked three miles to the next village you would know what sort of crops the good yeomen were growing, how well they looked after their animals, whether the outlying farms were built in a unified style. Then you might see how they all belonged to the same landlord. As you got closer, you might see how much wealth resided in that village and how it was distributed between the inhabitants. As you walked to the centre you would hear their voices and you might know whether or not they were people like you. You might meet people and they would tell you.

When you're driving it is all gone as soon as you've arrived. You might have time to see the names of the shops as you dawdle at the lights, but there is no time to realise fully the architectural delights of the parish church. At speed, everything is lost before it's begun, like the individual frames of a motion picture.

There are places I know from familiar journeys that are always transit places. I've never stopped in them, they are simply signposts on the route. I can never stop in them, because they are not actually, actually real. If I were ever forced to stop, I could never be still, because the incompleteness of the journey would be calling me on.

Most of this M1 I've only ever passed along – a conduit to other places. It might as well be a tube. I've stopped off at the various services from time to time, but they're not real. Sure, they have names like Watford Gap and Toddington which suggest real places, but they are just nodes on the conduit. The people who designed them know this, which is why you can't actually get off at services and interconnect with the rest of the universe. Instead, you find a sort of miniature model community with its own infrastructure – places to stay, places to eat organised in a hierarchy of cost, places to buy essential items, even its own Police force. It has its own controlled border and its own rules on where you can't go in your vehicle and when you're on foot. It even has a sort of 'behind the scenes' which you don't get to see. On the surface it's like the thing you'd get if someone from the future had recreated our time using only information from hoardings.

My packed lunch breakfast had all but boiled off. Sometimes you need a proper meal. Driving on my sort of schedule doesn't often allow for that, especially with hold ups: now I was getting bogged down around the exit to the M42. Gigi was on the radio again, telling me about delays on the M180. Obviously this set of stuff wasn't featuring on her radar.

The drizzle had turned to spray. The spray must have been full of road salt, because I was having to wash a grey film from the screen every thirty seconds. Clouds from cooling towers by the roadside were drifting towards me – the whole thing a conspiracy to keep me in the dark.

After I lost my job everything went blank. Not blank as in memory loss, but blank as in featureless. As each day passed there was nothing to stub my foot on as much to say that something happened. Each day slid away without note. I had felt something like this before, some time ago, but this time it had a sort of millennial flavour about it.

I never knew what was supposed to happen after the end of the century. It was something you looked forward to, but not beyond. All the literature was about life in the year 2000, how we were going to live, how we would have to solve our food problems and the challenges of a burgeoning population. It was about technological advances, cities under the sea and longterm communities on the moon, silver suits and electronic pop music, even though that's already in the past. The old millennium has passed and we're just half way through the first decade of the new one. No one suggested what it might feel like to drift planless, through a nondescript life, with no money, in one of the most expensive cities in the world.

I hung up my leathers and sat in my flat day after day. All my momentum had been caught up in the bike. When I sold the bike to pay the rent the momentum went with it. Most of the time I counted the hours until I could convince myself that going to the pub was the best available option to stop me counting the hours.

That was it. I couldn't say I was becoming a drunk, because I couldn't afford to drink that much. There were probably other things to do, but at the same time as I lost my job I suffered a failure of the imagination. Maybe that had happened even before I lost the job, but I'd been too busy to notice. In the same way, I hadn't seemed to notice that I didn't have any friends outside of work. In fact, I don't suppose I'd noticed anything happening to me for a long time. My life had just got small and the mechanism by which that had happened had passed me by. Each day I sat around the flat, went to the little supermarket to get something to eat, watched anything on the television to stave off feelings of wanting to go to the pub, gave in and went to the pub. Eventually even the television gambit disappeared. I still watched, but I knew that I would be in the pub by half-nine at the latest. Drink, back home after closing, fall asleep at three, wake up at six and go to bed, sleep in until late and start the whole cycle over again. With a routine like that you can get through a whole chunk of life without it hardly registering.

By this time I should have been well past Nottingham.

Every fucker in the East Midlands must have been converging on this one stretch of the M1 for an afternoon of sprayday frolics. Didn't they know I was running late for an appointment? Didn't they look out of their windows before setting off and ask themselves what the hell they wanted to be doing out on a day like this? A shit day in December is no time to be committing yourself to the road. That's for we poor fuckers who don't have a choice.

Junction 25. I looked over to the southbound carriageway. I looked back at my own. I made allowances for the fact that the other side generally looks better than yours and guestimated the extra burden on my carriageway. Meadowhall – they're all going Christmas shopping. Ten thousand amateurs rolling up to Sheffield for the annual festival of retail therapy. I'd be on and off the brakes for the next fifty miles.

There are several categories of driver. About forty percent of the total are your Competents. These are people who drive most days, have driven in a range of conditions on a range of different types of road. They've gained some reasonable experience, they may even have a lifetime of driving behind them. They can adapt to most situations that arise. Most of the time these people don't cause you any problems. Some go too slow, some too fast, but most know that you don't do anything to upset your fellow road users.

If you arrange the Competent to form a scale, at the upper and lower extremities you find the Ultra Violet and the Infrared. The Ultra Violet are your omni-competents. These are people to whom driving is an art. They may hold an advanced driving qualification. They certainly have pride in their standard of driving and their consideration for other road users. They've driven in most conditions and they've driven different types of vehicle. They keep up with road conditions on the open road and they go carefully in urban areas. They know about car maintenance. They may even check their tyre pressures once a week. They never cause problems on the road.

Your Infrareds are your thrash merchants. They think they know what they're doing, but in fact they're sliding off the bottom of the competence scale. They probably have a good measure of car control when they're smoking tyres around some housing estate, but they don't know where speed is appropriate and when it's not. They drive full on or full off. These are people who will cut you up, drive up your arse, stamp on the brakes, pass you regardless of circumstances, drive on ego alone. They are of either gender, are usually young, but can be of any age. Usually, they don't venture too far from where they've come. If you encounter them on the motorway they're usually just hacking along for a couple of junctions. You can spot them a mile off. If possible, it's best to stay out of their way but, if you're having a bad day, you can guarantee to find one.

There's your Professionals, falling into several subdivisions of their own: truckers (long and short haul), light goods (such as myself), reps of all kinds, service staff who have to drive as part of their job, including maintenance engineers and professional trouble shooters, vehicle delivery operatives, cab drivers, bus and minibus drivers, including those transporting work gangs, military drivers and, of course, all members of the emergency services. There are also lots of minorities, such as people who drive in contained environments like quarries and airports, but they maintain their professional status even when they're driving to and from work. Amongst these you do get rogues and people having an off day but, for the main part, you're better off driving amongst professional types during the cut and thrust of the working day. All the wagons and trailers and stuff may be bunging up the roads, but they're not all that likely to bung you into a ditch.

Then there are your Amateurs. The Competent are, in fact, amateur, but they're not the same as the 'Amateurs'. Amateurs shouldn't really be on the road without a chaperone. They may be people who drive every day: two miles to work; 1200 yards back and forth on the school run; down to the shops on a Saturday; over to the in-laws once a fortnight. The most competent of them might know how to top up the oil, but they will never know what's inside a gearbox. They come out in hordes during the holiday season for their sole annual trip of more than twenty miles. As soon as they've driven out of familiar territory they become bewildered and sit, staring slack-jawed in their driving seats, hunched over the steering wheel. Many are urban drivers who can muster fifty in a thirty zone but can't top forty-five once they're on the motorway. The normal rules of engagement for the modern motorist are a mystery to them. You'll think they've become a fixture in the central lane and then they'll suddenly move over when traffic is joining without indicating or even checking their mirror. They'll take their eyes off the road to talk to their passenger or even turn round to shout at the kids. You'll see them putting their seatbelts on long after they've set off. They'll drive with under-inflated tyres and terminally worn-out dampers. They'll cover the dashboard in food cartons and block off the ventilation. They'll pull out at junctions without looking; they'll stack up a fifty car queue behind them in perfect oblivion. Worst of all, they'll all come out simultaneously on a shit December day under the pretext of a trip to a shopping mall and block up the fucking road when I'm running late for my drop.

DAVE

If you have anything about you there's only so long you can do nothing. If you do nothing long enough, then it becomes impossible to resist the compulsion to do something. If you try to resist then you'll end up feeling like you'll do anything.

So there was a natural limit to how long I could continue with my lying-in-late, pub-in-the-evening routine. After three months, having conjured up all the options of what I'd like to do and rejected them as unrealistic, I took a day and did a round of the despatch offices. I got my hair cut and had a shave and put on my leathers to look the part.

No one was hiring, or rather, they weren't hiring anyone without a bike. Yes they'd bought bikes for riders before, a fleet of nice, shiny Kwakkers when they first set up. Two riders fucked off with theirs in the first week, one claimed that his got 'stolen' and three others dropped theirs and trashed them within a fortnight, 'Riders adopt a cavalier attitude if they're not on their own machine.'

Still, I went round every office. By the time I'd finished it was dark and late and a neon sign saying 'pissed off' was flashing before my eyes. I got on the bus and rode, in incongruous style, to a wild-west pub that some of my old despatch friends had told me about. I'd never been, because it didn't sound like my kind of place, but I figured it might be worth it if it could get me the inside picture on any vacancies. None of them were there.

I stood at the bar, creaking in my leathers, looking unintentionally mean because of my mood. It was probably best I was on my own, even if I was drinking too fast.

Somewhere between pints two and three I had a proper look around and realised I had pitched up in an example of the worst sort of sticky-floored dive. Perhaps my compadres patronised the place because it was the only sort of place that would let them in, being bikers and all.

I passed my eyes briefly over the clientele. Gold chain and indistinct tattoos. The air smelled of cigar and the dry cough-mixture of exhaled cigarette smoke. As luck would have it no one noticed I was looking at them – these were not the sort of people who take being looked at lightly. When I got back to myself it was clear that it was my turn. Around the corner of the bar, from a dark space between the quiz machine and the hand pumps, a pair of dim eyes were watching me. A thin hand rose towards them and they opened wide to draw in smoke from a matchstick roll-up that must have been mostly paper. Ex con, I thought, only an ex con would roll a fag that thin.

I drank my dregs and ordered another one. However uncomfortable I was feeling in the place, I wasn't in a mood for giving in, so I took my time. When I looked up again dim-eyes was still watching me. Perhaps he was trying to psyche me out. I concentrated on putting myself at ease. Then he started to move. He slid off his stool to demonstrate how short he was and came towards me around the corner of the bar.

Shit, I thought, he's going to come round and talk to me. There must have been just that bit too much eye contact and he's taken it as an invitation.

He kept his eyes on me all the way, alternating between a point just below my neck and the full pint in my hand. That's it, he wants me to buy him a drink. I thought about knocking it back and making a swift getaway, but he was almost on me. I was just getting resigned to the fact and preparing for the inevitable invasion of my personal space, when he inexplicably changed course and headed for the door. The stub of his roll-up dropped to the floor and continued to smoke merrily away on the greasy mat of the carpet. Neither customer nor staff seemed to care. The same went for me. There must have been so much ground-in dirt and spillage in that carpet that it had long exceeded the possibilities of flammability. I started my pint.

About half way through drinking it I noticed that old rat-fingers had returned. He was a presence behind me, making my skin shudder. I watched him go back to his crevice by the quiz machine. He cast a glance back to my side of the bar, but he wasn't looking at me, he was looking at the guy next to me.

He was a broad-shouldered man of around forty, with a shaven head attempting to disguise the fact that he was going bald. He may have been thirty – there was no way of telling. At least he was smiling, if you could call it that. His expression might have been the sardonic grin of one who is about to do you incalculable harm. He hadn't said anything, but the barman was already busy mixing up some kind of drink for him that came in a tall glass. In any case, it was me he was looking at.

'You a biker, yeah?'

I suppose it was obvious, but I never like to be rude, 'Yes, you could say that.'

'Yeah, love bikes me, Hondas and that, what are you drinking?'

'Thanks, but I haven't finished this one yet.'

That wasn't the right answer.

'Oi Carl, get him another one of whatever he's havin' will ya?'

Carl the barman placed my new friend's drink on the bar top and started to pull me another pint. I didn't bother to argue – the thing seemed to be a *fait accompli*.

'Bikes, yeah, what you call 'em, Suzukis. My brother had one of them, always in the yard fucking about with it. Didn't half fucking go though, when it was working. What's your name?'

'Ben.'

'John?'

I didn't really want to tell this effusive, somewhat threatening looking geezer what my name was, or anything about me. I just told him before I had thought about it, but as chance had it the jukebox had chosen that very moment to strike up a tune and drown out my response.

'Yes, John.'

It was a simple mis-hearing, but from then on I was John. John is easy; you still get called it when someone hasn't got a handle for you or if they're inclined towards the generic. It's a cliché and it's going out of style, but you still hear it said: 'All right, John?' and 'Oi John, you want tickets? Half price.'

'Okay John, you can call me Dave.'

He said it as if it was one of many names he might go under, but it was apparent that this one was genuine: it said DAVE on his big gold ring.

'Thanks for the drink, Dave.'

He was looking up and down my leathers and I was beginning to wonder whether he had designs. In my book a stranger doesn't come out of the blue and buy you a drink for no good reason, particularly in a shite-hole like this one. Dave took a sip from his cocktail and licked his lips. 'Nice.'

Things weren't so good then. Now I had my half-pint and another full one. There was no easy way of drinking up and making an escape without looking like a prat or, worse, giving affront to a bloke with a signet ring the size of a pound coin.

'Watcha do then John? You a courier or something?'

I don't know why I felt suddenly compelled to tell him. Perhaps it was because I had been brought up to be polite and he had bought me a drink, perhaps it was because I couldn't see how he could use the knowledge to his advantage.

'I used to ride despatch, up until a couple of months ago, now I'm a bit underemployed.'

'You don't say.' His mind was ticking over something while he took another couple of sips. 'Tell you what John, why don't you join me in my office?'

His office turned out to be a table in the darkest corner of the pub. We had to pass rat-fingers to get there, but he wasn't interested in me anymore. He did acknowledge Dave though, raising his glass of beer a little and giving a nod.

I sat down with Dave in his quiet corner, sure that events were about to unfold that would inevitably lead to me undergoing an experience that I might, sooner rather than later, regret. Instead, he offered me a job.

'But I haven't got a bike.'

'Don't worry about that. We can get you a bike. We just need you to do these deliveries. Well it's not even deliveries, it's more like taking a message, all big companies. You know your way around, yeah?'

If I knew anything, I knew my way around.

'It's easy stuff John, but it's all over.'

Puzzling – Dave didn't strike me as the sort to run a despatch business, not despatching packages anyway.

'Look, how much were they paying you?'

I don't much like to discuss money, but I told him down to the last penny. Then I told him about overtime rates and special bonuses. I didn't even exaggerate. Dave took it all in.

'Well fuck that, we'd be looking at triple. We might even be looking at a profit share.'

'What sort of profit forecasts are we talking about?'

The loss of the bike and two months of comparative penury had made money an abiding issue. In fact I was desperate. Dave had access to money: his gold told you that.

My question had obviously amused him, because his torso was bouncing up and down in time to a series of gruff chuckles, 'Let's just say that the forecast is good eh? Fuckin' good.'

I knew there was something irregular about the whole set-up. I also knew that without money I was going to slip into the shit. I'd been sacked, so there was going to be no dole for some time. I had given notice on my flat and there was no going back. Even if I could pay the rent, I had once got behind and I hate being thought of as trash. I was out because of two months of arrears. I even told Dave that, because he asked where he could get in touch.

'Fuck it, look, take some of this and get yourself sorted out.'

He took a big wedge of cash out of his pocket and reeled off a load of twenties. I saw him count off twenty-five. He folded them up and pushed them into my hand. I took them with a certain relish, even though my brain was saying, 'What the hell are you doing?'

'There you go, call it an advance.'

'Dave, thanks and all, but we've only just met. How do you know you can trust me?'

He gave me a 'does not compute' look before pocketing the remainder of his wedge, 'Well, you're not going to take what I give you and fuck off, are you?'

The only possible answer to this was 'no'.

'No,' I said.

PHONEY

The scam worked like this: I started out each morning from the dingy workshop that served as headquarters for Dave and his partner Terence. The workshop must once have held a thriving car repair business, but that was long gone. Now it was a quiet backwater where no one came, even though it was situated behind a busy high street.

I had a list for the day and a mobile phone for emergencies. I had a new helmet and a new 600cc sports bike they had found me from somewhere (I didn't ask). In truth the bike was not really suitable, what with its head-down riding position, but it was a nice ride all the same. I had a satchel, with the logo 'Red Couriers' on it. In the satchel I carried a dozen or so A4 jiffy bags each addressed to an employee at a different company. Not that all of these were guaranteed to get delivered on the same day – it depended how time went.

I rode all over London, to each of the addresses on my list, just like my old job, only this time there was no abuse coming through the headset and there was nothing to pick up. At each drop I parked up and went into reception.

'Package for Mr Bultitude.'

'Package for who?'

'Er Bultitude, look.'

I showed them the name on the package, the same name repeated on the delivery note.

'Okay, just leave it there.' Then they'd sign.

Sometimes it would happen like that and you'd be forced to turn tail and leave. Mostly though, receptionists don't behave like that. For a start, they don't want a steaming biker covered in road filth standing in reception, making the place look unreceptive – that's *their* job. Also, they don't get to wield power over anyone else, so they go out of their way to wield it over scum like myself. More often than not, then, the discussion would continue:

'There isn't anyone here by that name.'

'Look, I've got this package for Mr Bultitude. This is the right company, yeah?'

I showed them the delivery note. The company details were always correct.

'Yes but we don't have any Bultitudes.' (Only bad attitudes)

'Either way, this is marked urgent, perhaps they've got the name and the company mixed up. You got a phone?'

By this time you're leaning over their desk and people are queuing up behind you.

'Haven't you got a mobile or a radio?'

'Look lady, I only want to use the phone. I'll only be a minute, then I can sort this out.'

'All right, use that one there. Press nine for an outside line.'

Only then did I take my helmet off, but I always had my thermal balaclava on underneath, and I was always careful to turn away from the receptionist.

'Thanks…Hello, Despatch?…yes, it's me…what?…yes, I'm here now…well get him then…(thirty seconds pass)…no…they're telling me there's no one here by that name…no…yes…it's the right address…yes, I'll hold…(as many seconds as you think you can get away with)…okay, will do.'

Put down the phone and appear pissed off. 'Look I'm sorry love, they've messed it up at despatch. Sorry to bother you. Thanks for the use of the phone, yeah?'

Put your helmet back on and leave with the package.

There was no one on the other end of the line, only an answering machine. The number I dialled was to an offshore premium line – you can set what premium you want. I don't know what Terence and Dave had settled on – five hundred pounds a minute, a thousand? I'd try and make each call last at least two minutes, if the receptionist was busy, three or four, or whatever I could get away with.

How often does a big company check its phone bill? Does anyone even notice when there's a huge call charge to a single number? Does a business with perhaps five hundred phone lines and twenty-four hour online connection even care? Who knows?

Whatever, Dave and Terence must have been coining

it in. They paid me what Dave had said, and some more. I got myself a new flat and a couple of things to make it more comfortable. I knew I was doing something wrong, but somehow the money made it possible.

Everything was tight and professional. Terence had seen to it. My helmet was sprayed with the company logo; the delivery notes were printed up with the same. As a money-spinning angle it was very hard to spot, but it had to stop. Terence had a master list that was supposed to keep us busy for three months, which it did. Then we walked away. I was pleased because I had some cash. I thanked Mr Bultitude daily.

I only met him once. What are the chances of that? Bultitude is a rare name, you only have to look it up in the phone book to see that. But one day I asked for him and he was there.

'Mr Bultitude? I'll call him down for you.'

I wasn't prepared for that. Not that it mattered. I handed over the package and he signed for it. A shame really, a nice, youngish man like that, probably recently married, doing his best for the company. He'd get back to his workstation in the carrel he shared with three other people and open the package and deposit two hardcore porn mags onto his desk.

It was my idea. There was a stack of the stuff in the workshop. I figured that if a package got accepted and opened at reception it would look as if some geek in the company had ordered it over the internet under an assumed name. No one would own up to a thing like that, so it would make the delivery appear legitimate. Terence liked the idea and it got rid of some of the stack of out-of-date porn.

I suppose that, if we had kept it up, at some point someone would have made the connection and I would have turned up at a drop to find that the staff were wise, or, come out afterwards and find the Police waiting by my bike. My new employers pitched the time-scale just right.

Dave and Terence weren't bothered that it was just short term – the purpose of the game wasn't to make a mint and retire to the south of France, it was to accrue capital for the acquisition of stock.

CLOWNE WOODS

There's a certain satisfaction to be gained from motorway travel when it's moving along. It's something to do with the way that constant motion removes you from the world of static realities. To the question, 'Where are you?' the reply is, 'M1 heading north, between junctions 27 and 28.' Such an answer does not denote a location, it suggests an idea; 'heading north', 'westbound' and 'on the downhill stretch' are abstracts with connotations of a state of mind. They are statements of intent. The motorway is a funnel of intent bending those abstracts of will into tightly controlled strands, holding them there until the will exhausts itself at the point of destination.

Motorway is the opposite of destination. Even road workers replacing worn-out blacktop are moving on in their own, pedestrian way.

There are two types of tarmac: fast and slow. You would think that fast is the one that would need the greater strength, the higher resilience, but the reverse is true. Slow is reserved for approaches to junctions and places where wagons sit heavy in the same place for the longest time. Here the spot pressures are at their greatest.

On fast sections the weight has come and gone before its effects are felt; the movement distributes the pressure. On the modern motorway many fast sections have become slow and are feeling the effects.

The motorway mind is free from realisation: all that comes up is quickly left behind. Anticipation becomes memory without anything in-between. The motorway leaves you alone with yourself and the inside of your car. Everything else is a flux of the part-perceived and the impermanent. Because it's all ephemeral, you look to what is not: the inside of your car and the inside of yourself. The road, in a way, gives you access to your soul.

I'm not suggesting that our motorways are nose to tail with solipsistic existentialists, just that you are never quite as alone as when you are alone in the car. That's why I often prefer to leave the radio off and why, sometimes, I have to have it on.

I have two bottles of wine in my overnight bag: one for tonight and one for tomorrow. Dawn will be pleased to see what I've brought; I don't know about the other.

I am doing seventy-five, on my way to drop two, trying to make up time. I want this last trip to go well, but I'm also feeling the pressure of time. Time is a dictator running a dirty-tricks campaign. Time is all you have, yet you are never allowed to keep it. In the timetable of events you have to rush to consume as little as possible, yet the rushing makes the time go quicker and you feel like, rather than getting where you wanted sooner, you have wasted time instead.

This driver has little choice. Regardless of the outcome, I am going to drive around. In a little over fifty hours I'll be back. This time for the last time.

I've gone from thinking about Dawn's wine in the overnight bag to Gail. I am counting the time we spent together back then and finding it hard. It's not just the remoteness in time that's causing the problem, it's more the lack of time and the fact that I didn't think it might need to be quantified. If you knew that something was finite you might tick off the minutes as slowly as you could, holding each moment in your hand, gripping it tighter until it was torn from your grasp. But you do know it's finite and still you rush at seventy-five, trying and failing to make time.

It was early afternoon. The diesel in the tank was going down, but not to the point where I was going to have to do something about it. I prefer to fill up at cheaper places away from the motorway. I'm not paying, so it's not my money I'm saving. It's the principle of the thing.

The afternoon was as dull and damp as the morning, but now a northern wind was cutting across the carriageways. I could feel the extra chill through the air vents. I was feeling hungry, but there was no time to stop and snack.

I'd been counting off the landmarks: Hucknall Chimneys; Tibshelf Services; Bolsover castle. This was the drop I liked best, the only one with an air of mystery.

It was more than two and a half years since the route had been a three-day affair; this drop had been on from the start.

I left the motorway at Junction 30 and took the A619 towards Worksop past Clowne. When I retire from the circus I will live in Clowne. In the evenings I will Shuttlewood to Bolsover and drink Langwith Scarcliffe until we are Wellbeck Abbey. That's when I retire. For the moment I must get onto the small road and find the gated wood.

I turned off the engine and got out. Each time I'd come here I'd felt that someone was watching me. It made me think that if I paid attention to the silence I might be able to hear them rustling about.

How had Terence organised this with the customer? I knew little about the ins and outs of procedure, I was merely sent out to do the job.

It's odd really, because there are only three of us in the operation, but then I am very much the outsider. I certainly can't complain about the money. Since the inception of the three-day route I've had more money than I know what to do with, and I'm not usually short on ideas. Too many ideas and not enough plan – perhaps that's it.

I lifted the chain from the gatepost and opened up a gap. The gate dragged on the ground, it's back broken by the weight of sodden wood.

There was only one carton to drop. There was only ever one, regardless of the intervals between drops. I walked amongst the mud and leaves carrying it against my chest.

The woods were crowded out, darkened with ivy. Perhaps the customer possessed a sense of the melodramatic. I listened for signs of life, but there was nothing but my box and me. I reached the tree with the big cleft at the root and pushed the box inside.

When I was a kid I used to walk with Mum in a place called Caesar's Camp. The woods there were dank and lively and full of history to be felt. I looked out for signs of tents and the armour of ancient soldiers, even though I knew those things were too long ago to have left visible marks. Still, there was a ghost of the place. Caesar's Camp had ghosts that predated the soldiers. I could feel that every time we went there.

Every journey has its stops. In the Camp I always stopped by the hollow tree. It had a vent in its side like an opening eye, as if the tree had unzipped itself to show that it was empty inside. Toadstools fed on the emptiness, the only visible manifestation of the wood-spirit ghost. It was like looking into a form of deathness, something with a greater truth and meaning than the small life that I was carrying inside. The more I looked, and I always looked for as long as I could manage, the more I realised the connection between the two. Behind the newness of myself was a thin strand that led back to this spirit thing. More than this, when my newness had turned to oldness and crumbled away, the wood ghost would remain. Perhaps the thin strand would draw me back into the hollow tree and the trunk would close up again.

There was no sign on the muddy ground around me that anybody had been there for some time. Once, I had driven up the road and waited to see if anyone arrived at the entrance to the gated wood, but no one came. Perhaps the tree consumed the box; perhaps it was Terence paying his tithe to the Devil.

I scraped the mud and leaves from my boots as best I could on the rotting gate and stared back into the wood. The ivy would choke everything in time, but I wouldn't be there to see it. There were never going to be answers at this drop, a fact I rather liked.

My muddy feet were slipping on the pedals, so I opened the window and turned up the heat to dry them out. I was keen to get back onto the motorway and into the flow again, especially as I had taken more time than I'd thought. I dropped a cog and gunned it a little, up to the 57 and back on at Junction 31, straight into a tailback for the M18.

GAIL

I didn't know until recently, but I have a photograph of Gail. I didn't think I had pictures of her from that time, but it dropped out from between the pages of my copy of *Twelfth Night* while I was throwing out the last of my old textbooks. Summer was leading into autumn.

Of course, I hadn't thought about her for years. I hadn't thought about anyone for years. That was part of the deal. I'd made sure there wasn't anything around that made me think of things. Autumn leads to winter and you find yourself on your last trip.

I was looking at the photograph as if for the first time. I had no memory of it. I couldn't have taken it, because I've never owned a camera. Gail couldn't have taken it, because she's on it. And it's not really 'of' her, it's of a group of students singing outside a city-centre shop. They are singing carols for Christmas on behalf of the college. Gail is on the left of a group of four, holding up a book of music. Her mouth forms an oval. The sound that she is making has been lost to time, but the likeness of her survives. It occurs to me that this is the only actual image of Gail that I have ever had in my possession.

I think of all those posed photographs from the

nineteenth-century, in which a gentleman amateur has captured examples of useful toil, for the subject a once-in-a-lifetime opportunity to be recorded for posterity. A group of lead-workers stand outside a storage shed, holding the tools of their trade, staring at the camera as they have been asked to do. The most interesting thing of all is the relationship between photographer and workmen: I will capture the essence of your soul, because I have the power to do so, I have the leisure to make it possible.

Gail makes an 'O' with her mouth. I know that she is singing, but now there is no sound; the image carries on to the present without its life. She looks from the photograph; I look back. She is at the edge of what is going on. In the direction she is looking, I will be at the periphery of her vision. Even across this field of unconnection she has a message for me that the mute photograph cannot convey. If this were the moving frames of celluloid or the feed of magnetic videotape I might stand a chance. As it is there is just an enigmatic, frozen glint of light refusing all attempts at decryption.

I leaf through *Twelfth Night* to see if there are any more images. I scrabble through every book to see if I have hidden a library of photographs and forgotten all about them but, of course, there are none.

Then it's later and I'm back on the road. Alone in the van even the photograph of Gail is a memory and I'm wondering if my mind's eye has it pictured just right. I'm faced with the dilemma that all I have is a memory of a memory whose only substance is the electrical discharges of synapses and chemical reactions between tissues. It's all becoming very remote and, of course, by continually thinking it through, I'm adding to the weight of memory. Gradually, the few concrete details are getting buried under piles of hearsay and re-thinking. There is no new evidence; it can only ever be new ways of looking at the old facts.

I remember I was sitting with Nick in the foyer of the new building at the college. It couldn't have been too long after Christmas in my last year. Probably – I forget – we had left a lecture and were waiting for a seminar, otherwise we would have gone elsewhere. That must have been it, because all the chairs in the café overspill area were full. That's why we were sitting on the low wall of the planter at the bottom of the stairs. The planter contained only gravel and doubled as an ashtray. I bet it's a no-smoking building now. Maybe it wasn't even a planter, just a bed of decorative gravel. Maybe it wasn't even gravel, just a textured surface, but we were certainly sitting there, beneath the stairs, facing the entrance door.

Gail came in. I can't say what for – she did different subjects to me and was in a different year. I knew that she knew Nick, but then Nick knew most people. I can tell you that she was wearing those black leggings, but I'm not sure whether she had on that olive denim jacket. I'm sure she came straight up and started talking to Nick. What about? I'm too preoccupied with the shape of her and the manner in which that shape is expressing itself to make a note of the conversation. She has an easy way with words and her posture is direct. Though she is talking to Nick she has not excluded me. That's polite, because in a way it could be said that she has intruded on the conversation between Nick and me. That's interaction. In the spirit of things I add something myself. Now it's three-way, albeit I'm the minority contributor. I can see now that she must have had a bag of books and stuff. She adjusts it on her shoulder. Soon she will go off to a lecture, or whatever. The event is just a few minutes long. I forget what I did next.

'You never know when you are making a memory,' someone once said. That's not strictly true. If someone stops you in the street, mugs you at gunpoint and makes a point of pistol-whipping you to facilitate their getaway, you can be sure you're going to remember that. If, however, it happened once a week on a Friday lunchtime, after a while you might not be able, in memory, to distinguish one attack from the next. This is all hypothetical, however. Out of the myriad, prosaic incidents of everyday occurrence you can't tell what's going to stick. Some say, of course, that everything sticks, the memory can be considered infinite. That's the theory to which I subscribe. Not all stuff, though, is amenable to recollection. What we call memories are the things that can be brought to the surface at will or after a few moments' meditation. So, out of the uneventful stuff, you can't tell what the memories are going to be and, in the long term, which are going to stand the test of time.

When I see Gail coming in, she has seen, through the glass of the door, Nick. Nick she knows. Who is he talking to? Me. Me she knows of, has seen. When Gail comes through the door she sees *us* and comes to talk. We will be a group of three. Because Nick is close in conversation with me I will be engaged in whatever she has to say. In the normal run of etiquette it would be difficult for her to come up to me, alone, and start to talk. She comes to talk when there is someone else she knows. Once the precedent is set she can come up and talk to me another time even if I am on my own.

That's the conclusion I draw, re-running the frames of the film to review the evidence. I draw in the history of her intent and the fact that she had an interest in me. I can see how she used the opportunity by way of an introduction. I test the theory again and again against the memory film and find that it holds up. In the absence of evidence to the contrary, it has to.

When I was nineteen, and on my own in the house with my parents out, I got trapped in the cupboard under the stairs. I was searching for the box of baby shoes, looking to amuse myself with comparisons of size. Would the sight of the tiny shoes trigger memories of me wearing them? I couldn't find them: perhaps my unsentimental father had thrown them out.

I should have known to move the ironing board from where it was propped against the open door. In a fit of pique it slipped down, closing the door on its way and wedging itself between the bottom of the door and the wall opposite the stairs. I tried to force it open, but it wasn't going to budge without damage. As I was in a state of non-gratis with my parents at the time, I thought discretion would be the better part of valour. I settled myself in for the long haul. There was no bulb in the socket, but there was heating, courtesy of a pipe-run through to the kitchen. I made myself comfortable on a nest of coats and Granddad's old, down sleeping bag and waited. It was late afternoon, late in the year and soon even the thin strip of light around the doorjamb disappeared with the evening sun. I sat in sensory deprivation with nothing to do.

In the warm air the only things I could see were images from memory. With so much time I could look as closely as I liked. There was the house we lived in when I was seven, the sandpit and the pampas grass in the neighbour's garden. There was the front door and the first steps on the route to school. In the undergrowth by the rail embankment the dumped bag of cement, hardened into a single block like a fossil, the bag rotted away. The tunnel under the railway, across from the shop where we got sweets on the way home, toadstools bubbling pneumatically through the black tarmac. Over the canal bridge and carefully across the highway to the swings singing '*far far away.*' Up the field to the school, counting the steps to the classroom, seeing the colour of the door, the layout of the chairs and tables and where the clock is in relation to the blackboard. That's where they keep the toys. This one consists of plastic squares and cylinders that can slot together into structures. Individually seeing the transparent colours and the way the assembly slots are configured on each piece. Now the striations and cracks developed by years of heavy-handed use. See all these things and more that haven't been seen or thought about since that time as clear, as the saying goes, as if it were yesterday.

That's why I feel that things are retained. If all the information in all the libraries in all the world can fit into a piece of brain the size of a pea, how much space does it take to store a lifetime of thoughts, sights, sounds and smells? Can you get at it all, if only you have the time and a dark, warm cupboard under the stairs?

WOOLLEY EDGE

The tow truck on the inside lane smelled of axle-grease. It reminded me of Terence and Dave and the workshop. Few people came to visit us there. If there was anyone to see, the boys liked to go out and do it elsewhere. If there was some pub or club where these things went on, they didn't tell me.

Ratfingers came in a couple of times, always keeping his distance from me, eyeing me suspiciously as if he had dobbed me in for something and was expecting revenge. He always smoked those stick-thin roll-ups and let the ash drop to the floor.

Then there was Specca. In the weeks after we put paid to the scam, he paid us an increasing number of visits. He wore big-framed glasses, but I don't think his moniker originated from that. It was a corruption of some given name but, like most things in the workshop, I wasn't privy to it.

I think he was like my opposite number in some other organisation. He looked at me as if I was shit, so I assumed there must be some competitive element to it. Whoever employed him let him drive around in crapped-out old 2.3 Granada. I had my sports bike, so perhaps it was that. He was as tall as me, wiry-looking, with slightly bulging eyes amplified by the lenses of his glasses.

He was coming round because there was something going on. Terence knew him of old, so I guessed the something had been bubbling under for some time. When Specca came in it was always, 'I've been sent to...' and 'We want to know...' whereupon he was shuffled into the office and out of my earshot. I tried not to speculate on what it was all about and took the money for the small tasks I was asked to complete. I had a new life where nobody asked me questions. I had sloughed off all weight of the past. Nothing was in my real name. I was John. Being John gave you a lot of latitude, because John wasn't responsible for anyone, not least himself.

Sometimes we took delivery of small packages; sometimes I took packages out. The packages were sealed when I got them and I didn't attempt to look inside. Usually I had to deliver them to some-or-other individual standing on a street corner, though two or three times I rode out to a superstore car park and handed them over to Specca. He received them with undisguised contempt. I couldn't blame him really: the rings on his old Granddad were shot and it bunny-hopped like mad away from rest. I slid off smoothly on my company bike, looking the part in my leathers. Still, it wasn't my fault.

I was leaving the smell of axle-grease behind. The tow

truck had turned off for the M18, while I continued up the M1. I switched on the radio exactly in time to hear Gigi with the traffic news. Too late she said, "Lorry jack-knifed on the M18 eastbound. Roger the Dodger says it's down to one lane up there and anyone on the eastbound carriageway should expect delays."

Great – if I'd known I could have stuck to the A57 and bypassed all the drama. If I'd have done a lot of things I could have bypassed all the drama but, with life's little eventualities, you're always getting the news just too late, eh Gigi?

I left the radio on for the music and tried to make the best time I could. Now that we'd been filtered through the blockage the traffic had thinned out. Makes you feel a little smug that you've done your time and can enjoy the benefits – at least until the next snarl up. I could do without any further delays. The heat from the foot well had dried me out and my hunger was being overtaken by thirst.

I wonder if I'd have stayed with Terence and Dave if I'd known? Probably, I like to see things through to the end. In fact these days I insist upon it. Lack of an ending leaves too many possibilities dangling in the air, like severed roots on an upturned tree felled by the wind. The unconsummated possibility can tease you for a lifetime. That's one reason I'm going to take this trip to its conclusion.

I found a space and touched ninety for half a mile. My thirst had been replaced by a complaining bladder and I regretted not having taken my opportunity in the woods. That's what happens when your mind's on other things. It was still only mid-afternoon, but ideologically a long way from the M25. Rotherham, Sheffield, Meadowhall, the disused cooling towers by the side of the road. The trip used to take me up the A1 past Ferrybridge where, in 1965, three of the eight towers blew down in a strong wind. The construction engineers had failed to take into account wind-sheer and turbulence in the lee of the closely spaced towers. There is a grainy picture of one of them, like a pole-axed giant, folding in on itself and coming down.

Dodworth, Barnsley, 'Gouranga' in pasted letters still on the footbridge above my path, Henry Moore's figures reclining in a field, out of sight of the road, the thin spire of Emley mast with its head lost in cloud.

I pulled into the services at Woolley Edge, thinking once again about sheep in a predicament, and looked around for a dark Nissan van. It was easily spotted, over at the far side of the car park, standing on its own, the merest hint of smoke rising from an open window. As I pulled alongside the source of the smoke got out.

'You're late, aren't you?'

'Traffic.'

'You're chuffin' jokin'. Bit of traffic. You want to start earlier.'

There was no point arguing – this drop was always the same. I tried to put it down to nerves on the part of my contact, but there was no escaping the fact that he was a nasty, sour piece of work with a sixty-a-day complexion. He was already getting a new fag out of the packet, even though the last one was two or three drags from being out. He turned those three into one, then reached into the van and put the butt in the ashtray. He freed the ashtray from its mounting, brought it outside the van and dropped the contents onto the ground. When I was younger I used to think that a big pile of dog-ends somewhere meant that someone had waited in one spot for hour after hour smoking steadily to pass the time, waiting for their true love to arrive, or, that they were perhaps engaged in some undercover operation. Now I know it for the supreme act of laziness it is. But why put your butt in the ashtray and then empty it on the ground? Why not just throw it straight onto ground anyway and cut out the middleman?

'You got the stuff then?'

Of course I've got the stuff. What would be the point of driving all this way if I haven't got the stuff? When have I not had the stuff?

'Yeah, your van open?'

'It's going in the front with me.'

'All right.'

He watched me go round the back. 'Going to take your time, are you?'

I wasn't going to take any more time than it took – I needed a piss. 'I'll take as long as I want.'

'You're a cheeky cunt. I'll bet your boss doesn't know you're like this.'

'I'm employed for my cheek.'

'Maybe I'll let him know.'

What did I care. I probably wasn't going to see this twat again. If he wanted it doing quickly he could do it himself, rather than standing there with a fag in his mouth, getting a light from a three-for-a-pound lighter. There were only two boxes – how long could it take?

Three minutes later he was gone and I was locked up again. Two minutes after that I was in the services sighing into the wall above a urinal and thinking about taking out a mortgage for a cup of tea and a sandwich.

CLASSIFIED

The M1 used to terminate in Leeds. When it was like that I used to picture all the traffic coming off at seventy and piling into the city, saturating the road system and backing up down the motorway. Perhaps people in the southern part of Leeds felt it was thus, but of course so much of the traffic would already have diverted, west to the Pennines, east to the North Sea ports.

Now there's the M1 extension, six lanes of concrete burbling your tyres as you sweep through a no-man's land of half-agriculture, half industrial decay.

It's a long way from London, the junction numbers in the high forties and the light of the day coming to an end. Then it's the A1: Bramham, Clifford, Boston Spa, Wetherby, Walshford, Knaresborough – making good time now it doesn't matter, catching the tail-end of the schools' rush and anticipating Dawn.

I settled in behind a four-by-four and slipstreamed for a while, imagining myself in a sea of calm. What was I going to say to her about it? Was I going to say anything? It felt like a long time since I'd seen her; it felt like a long time since I'd seen anyone except Terence and Dave and the few people that came and went at the unit. Perhaps Gail, but that didn't really count. There were no friends and family now, only myself and nine million other people in a city the size of a small state. Good to be on the road then, even for the last time – Boroughbridge, Ripon, Dishforth, off for the A19.

There's a lot to be said for operating with an assumed identity. As soon as I had said 'John' to myself enough times for the sound to become thoroughly familiar, that's who I was. I saw it the way a transvestite might see it: when Stuart is Sally the transformation is total. Sally is a discreet individual with her own needs, her own deportment, her own inflexions of speech, like Stuart's, but with a different accent. So I was John, who walked in the same way as myself, but was a little more hedonistic and used a shorter word where a longer one would do. If necessary, John could escape back to being Ben in his spare time. Thing was, though, there was no one around now who knew Ben, so there was rarely a need for him to surface at all. In fact, as John was getting away with things that Ben would never dream of, what was the point at all?

The possibilities were endless. I thought them through while lounging around in my new flat, conceiving the dramatic irony of me getting to know people while they knew nothing of who I really was. There were lots of far-fetched fantasies; I settled on personal ads.

It was all about having something to do on my two nights out. There's something I enjoy about checking into the cut-price motorway hotel, something about the anonymity of the room, the anodyne decoration and the depersonalisation of the processes that get you fed and get you a cup of tea. You don't get much in the way of service, but then you don't get that thing where there's always a member of staff in your face. In the motorway hotel you can be forgotten the moment you leave the front desk and not recollected until someone is sent to clean your room and change the sheets which would do for another two weeks if you were at home. I can get into that, especially with an absorbing read in the overnight bag, but less so when I've been thinking about some human interaction. Places like that are purely commerce driven, there is none of the sort of non-profit making addenda that make society interesting. More often than not they are situated miles away from that stuff. You can drive there to see it happening, but you will be a stranger when you arrive.

That's why I started with the personal ads. I kidded myself it was a social experiment, but really it was to take the edge off being alone.

The first day of my route was typically ending up around North Yorkshire/Cleveland area, so I started with a few of the papers around there.

It's all technical now and, like most things these days, seems to revolve around giving yourself an overweight phone bill. You phone up the special line and leave your twenty words of advertisement that are going to appear in the paper. Then you leave a longer, recorded voice message that people can access using the special number that appears at the bottom of your ad. Callers to that can leave their own message, which you can access by phoning up and entering the PIN number that was issued when you accepted the service. The ad people make their money by charging a premium rate for the phone calls. Quite a good service all round, really, if you don't want anyone to trace you back.

I took a long time thinking about snappy lines for my advert, things like, 'dedicated humorist seeks punchline,' before deciding that I needed to leave something innocuous if I wasn't going to exclude too many possibilities at too early a stage.

> Man, 6ft, dark, GSOH, 30 [close enough].
> Enjoys nights in, nights out, keeps trim,
> Drives. WLTM like-minded lady.

The voice message I left had more in a similar vein, only I tried to make my voice sound as if sex oozed from every pore. I probably came across as a stroke victim. Whatever – within a week I had a couple of dozen replies to choose from, including: 'Ee I hate these things, me…(click), 'I like the sound of your voice, but I can only see someone who puts animals first,' and 'When I looked at my chart it said that you were the one I'd been waiting for. This is fate.'

These, and a few others, I discarded out of hand. My trips were working out at about one every four weeks. I could arrange one meeting a month. Therefore I had to be selective.

The first was a disaster. The girl looked about sixteen and she'd brought two of her mates to the pub with her. They had obviously worked as a team before. Probably it was an evening's sport to them to step out in lightweight costumes and wind up some bloke who wouldn't be able to wring his attention away from their abundant cleavages. When it became apparent that I wasn't going to be up for that kind of juvenile fun they went a bit huffy and wanted to be taken out for a meal. I gave it some thought as one of them adjusted her micro-skirt and another let the spaghetti strap of her top fall from her shoulder, but I knew it was going to be too much trouble. I found an excuse to leave and let the image fuel a fantasy while I lay on my lonely hotel bed. It wasn't spending the money I minded, it was being taken for a ride.

The second meeting was little better. At least it was a one-to-one, though she wasn't the one I was expecting. She had told me she was tall and athletic, a message which must have lost something in the translation: she was a five-foot dumpling. Not that that was a problem, I just didn't like the misrepresentation. Also, she was nice enough in most respects, but I could tell that she wanted to be in charge. After an hour or so of matching me drink for drink I got the distinct impression that she had a game plan for how the evening was going to go down. I couldn't tell what that was, but I guessed from the way she was looking at me that it had something to do with revenge. I had never met her before, so I figured that the desire must have got transposed from somebody else. She was on the edge of her seat, clamming for something to happen. It wasn't sexual anticipation: I know the signs for that. No, she had a plan. I played it all night, until it was time to leave, said, 'Thanks for a good night,' and made a getaway. She got the message and didn't contact again. Later I wondered whether there might not have been some interest in the game after all and, later still that, of course, I was misrepresenting myself as well.

The third time I met Dawn. She came chaperoned by her sister, who stayed long enough to satisfy herself that I wasn't a lone-wolf killer, or perhaps long enough to memorise my features for the purposes of subsequent identification. She didn't say much about anything and within half an hour she was gone. Only then did I realise it was her voice that I had heard recorded on the message.

'Oh yeah,' said Dawn, 'Louise set me up. She thinks I'm in a bad relationship and keeps looking for ways to get me out of it. She doesn't live close enough to keep an eye on me so she thinks she's got to sort me out whenever she's up. That's why she's going for desperate measures.'

'I don't think I like being thought of as a desperate measure.'

'I don't mean it like that. She thought you sounded okay on the message thing. I only knew we were meeting someone once we had left the house; I thought it was girls' night out.'

'Well, you're here now. How about another drink? Or would you like to go somewhere else? Food, maybe?'

'They do food here. Louise said I was to stay put where she left me, so she knew what my last movements were.'

Louise had been watching too many real-crime programmes if she was coming up with lines like that. Still, I wasn't going to argue. Dawn wasn't the first face I'd pick out of a line-up of likely candidates, but she was good looking enough and had me interested for reasons I couldn't quite fathom. She was twenty-four and should have been a picture of radiant youth, but something had dulled her pallor. The way she was looking at me had a subtext of world-weariness and having been put through the mill. There was something to her and I was intrigued to find out what.

'You're not from around here then, John?'

'No.'

'So why put the ad in the paper?'

'To be honest I'm on the road most of the time, so one place is as good as another. This is the first time I've done this kind of thing, and they do say that northern girls are good for a laugh.'

That managed to elicit a fleeting smile.

'What do you do then? Salesman?'

'Not exactly. I do multi-drop delivery around the country. Every so often I wind up here, so I thought I'd make the best of it, you know, find some amenable company.'

'You're not shy, are you?'

John isn't shy. He doesn't have to be. 'If you're shy you don't make new friends,'

She wanted to go halves on the meal and I let her, not that I was bothered either way. I could see she was keen to be on equal terms, so keen that it made be suspect that she was making up for inequalities elsewhere. In any case, everything had gone all right. She had been polite all night, if a little guarded, and I had passed the time pleasantly enough. I think she thought I was all right and that the evening hadn't been a dead loss all round.

'Do you need a lift home?' I asked her.

'Louise said I shouldn't show you where I live, you could be any type of fucking lunatic.'

'Do I look like a lunatic?'

'Yes, a bit.'

'I'll walk you to a bus then. No, get a cab. I'll pay if you want.'

'You can drive me. I'm not going to get in a cab round here, you can't trust them.'

So I took her home to the nice little house that her mother had left her and we had sex on the living room carpet even before the last warmth had left our coffee cups. I wondered whether I should be letting myself go so soon, or whether this was the exact outcome I'd been planning for. Where was this going to lead? Was this any way to go about enjoying myself? As I was lying next to her in the old double-bed upstairs I decided to forget all these conundrums because all this was happening to John and he wasn't the sort to be bothered by that kind of stuff. After the two hours of fun and games that followed even Ben would have set aside his reservations, so it was a win-win situation.

Subsequently, we met every time I was up. It was my overnight stop. I would ring her to say I was coming and she would put off whatever else she was supposed to be doing. When I arrived she even let me put the van in her garage, which added to my peace of mind. Apparently, Louise had said that if I was all right on the first night I would be all right to go on with. So that was all right. Even so, the plan hadn't worked: she kept on hanging round with the guy she was with before.

He and a group of others had romanced her when she started going to pubs when she was sixteen. They were twice her age and on the lookout for opportunities like that (certainly that was the way I saw it). They taught her how to have a good time on pharmaceuticals and soon they were an intrinsic part of her life. She had slept with most of them, on and off, and been slapped around a couple of times for her trouble. She was seeing less of them now she was seeing me, but she couldn't leave it behind. I figured it was because they had got her young enough to convince her that this was as good as it got; she hadn't seen that there were other things to be had, or other ways of going about life that might be preferable. Still, the cracks were showing: she was talking tentatively about jacking in her job at the pet food hypermarket and doing something at college. I encouraged her by suggesting she rented out the house and went abroad for a while. She said, 'Why?' and I said, 'Travel broadens the mind.' She cogitated for a bit and then asked me where I lived, so I spun her a line about a shitty, run down block of flats and cockroaches and crime. 'That's why I spend my time on the road,' I told her, 'coming here is like a holiday.'

I did enjoy going. She was good company, even if the seedy side had left her with a black outlook on life. She also liked sex from a variety of angles, which suited me fine. And when we'd finished she always held on to me as if I was dearest thing in her existence and I was absolved from all guilt because she said it was right. Ben would have appreciated it, even if, on John, it was a sentiment lost. John let her see what he wanted her to see and, if that was acceptable to her, nothing more need be said. I kept going back and she kept wanting me back. I could even live with the fact that she was seeing someone else. I'd been to the clinic and there was nothing unwelcome coming my way. She was canny enough to know that there was no way he could know about me. I was her escape from all that. For that to work both things had to be kept separate. I would have liked her to make the separation permanent. I had enough regard for her to see that it would be in her better interest. Nevertheless, I wasn't going to go out of my way and do anything concrete about it. So on we went, ignoring anything that might make our liaisons seem less than satisfactory. In any case, for me, they were perfectly so.

STOCKTON

The Stockton drop was a straightforward enough thing. I got off the A19 and made my way to an unassuming newsagents at the corner of two terraced streets and stopped the van. The only thing that was odd was that I had been told never to talk to the man. Perhaps he thought that, if we hadn't ever exchanged words, then he would be somehow less traceable if the worst came to the worst. Perhaps he wanted to know as little about me as possible. It was skewed logic whichever way you looked at it: I knew the location of the shop, I knew what he looked like and, because the shop was an off-licence, I knew his name from the licensing information above the door.

Maybe the guy was trying to play the taciturn gangster, or something; he was in the shop when I went in, but he didn't even look me in the eye. It suited me anyway; one box dumped unceremoniously on the counter and straight out again, with plenty of time to prepare for meeting Dawn. As usual I went directly to the leisure centre.

I lay in the sauna for a long time with my eyes closed. For a while all I could see was motorway traffic, coming up behind me, passing me on the right, falling back on the left. I had dawdled through town traffic for a while after that, been to the shop, walked to and through the leisure centre, but I still hadn't quite come to a rest. The sauna was adjustment time, an opportunity to sweat out driving odours from my armpits and crotch. The van's air vents have a way of driving a film of road dirt deep into your pores. Meeting Dawn is best done when you are in control. You can get that feeling by getting clean and giving yourself time to relax, putting on one of John's pressed shirts and driving slowly over to the American Diner. There you can sit at the bar waiting for her to turn up, every so often lifting a bottle of Michelob to your dry lips while keeping a weather eye on the van parked outside.

'Hiya.'

It was Dawn. She didn't touch me, or sit down at the stool next to mine. She liked to play it cool to start with. That was her way of being in control, making it appear as if the whole thing was her idea.

I smiled a bit and raised an eyebrow, 'All right?'

'You going to buy me a drink then?'

I got her a drink: rum and coke.

'Been here long?'

'Fifteen minutes. No problem.'

'I couldn't get out sooner. They kept us all back for the Area Manager's presentation. They've got some fucking nerve. None of us get overtime. Why couldn't they do it in work's time? It was a load of bollocks anyway about restructuring and performance plans.

We've had it time and time again. They want us to implement stuff that will mean more work, but they don't want to implement any more pay. We end up doing what they say, but it doesn't work because some fucking accountant's never done the job has worked it all out. Six months later we have to go through the whole thing again… Sorry John, am I losing you? Good trip?'

'Yeah okay, bit of trouble on the M1, but nothing desperate. Anyway, you can forget about that now. We can have something to eat. Are you hungry? I'm hungry, big-time.'

The sauna makes you ready for salty food. Thirsty too. That beer hadn't touched the sides. I got us both another drink, even though she had barely started hers. I figured she might relax a bit more with another rum inside her. She drank up the first one so she wouldn't have to carry two to the table and asked me how it had been in the last month.

'You know, busy. I've been all over the shop, North Wales and Manchester dropping paperwork between offices, hardly a day at home.'

'Bet you're a bit sick of being on the road?'

'Well you know, when it rains. It's always fucking raining over there.'

How did I become so adept at lying? I don't even have to think about it now. I don't even feel as if I have to be consistent. I just say what I want without a tremor in my voice, without looking away, without sweating or playing with my hands. I wonder which one of us has cultivated this skill with such accomplishment. North Wales? I haven't been there since I was ten and on a family holiday in Llandudno. I haven't left the South East at all this month. I've been up to the unit a couple of times and I've dotted around on the bike. That's it. The rest of the time I've been drinking brandy and watching film after film on the DVD, re-spooling over the bits I like and only getting up for necessities.

I got back on to her, 'You're going to carry on putting up with your job then, even though they keep on doing stuff like this to you?'

'Unless they want me out. There's not too many jobs about and the money's all right.'

I know what they pay her and it's not. 'I still say you want to get some money together and go travelling. You could live for a month in the Far East on what it costs for a week here. You could get by on the rent if you let your house out.'

'No way.'

'Why not. There's so much to see and the weather's so much better than fucking Cleveland.'

'You ever been?'

'Couple of times, Goa, the Thai islands [I've never been further than southern Spain]. That's why I think you should go. It's a real eye-opener.'

'John would never let me go.'

It's often amused me that the idiot she's hanging around with when she's not hanging around with me is also called John. Not that I wouldn't prefer it if he was out of the picture altogether. 'The sort of bloke that gives cunts a bad name,' an old despatch friend of mine used to say. Crude, but occasionally appropriate in use. Dawn would be well rid of him and his lowlife mates. The amusing thing is the thought that, if she calls out my name in the middle of whatever bedtime pursuits they get up to, how will he know she's thinking of me? I've thought about it in on a number of occasions, but really I like to think of her with me.

'Bollocks to him. You don't owe him anything. If he wasn't so busy getting off his head and getting you to do the same he might realise that he's using you. You might realise that you're being used.'

'You don't know him.'

'Oh, I know him all right.'

'Anyway he doesn't use much stuff anymore and he does care about me. He'd never have gone out with me so long if he didn't.'

'Has he ever said so?'

'Well no, he doesn't need to say it.'

'Let me put it this way, would you like it if he did?'

'I suppose.'

'Then, if he knows you he should know what you're like, he should know what it is you'd want to hear. If he knows you well enough he must know how you like to be treated.'

The conversation was obviously pissing her off. Perhaps it was sounding too much like criticism. It wasn't meant to. It was meant to help. It was my last chance to be of any help at all. 'Anyhow, you should get away. Go for a month and see if you like it. Go for a fortnight if you want. Just get away from here.'

'They'd never let me off work.'

'There are times in your life when you just can't work.' Now I'm beginning to sound like Ben. Tonight I don't want to be a pain in the arse; it needs to be a bit special. A moment's thought.

Someone is sniffing around the van. Two lads who've recently pulled up in a Mark Two Golf with no ground-clearance. It's probably innocent, but I can't be too careful. Stand up and get a better look.

'What is it John?'

'Nothing, just a couple of lads. I've got some of the good stuff on again. It makes you a bit wary parked up anywhere.'

'Is there a bottle for me?'

'Don't you worry about that. Anyway, it's time for pudding.'

We both have something calorific with a quasi-American name and sit back, bloated, licking the remainder from the corners of our mouths. I've had two more beers and Dawn's wet lips are giving me ideas. I know I have to wait; the waiting is part of the pleasure.

'What do you want to do now then?' I ask, 'Want to go to a film? We could go clubbing if you want.'

'Christ, not midweek. Why don't we go to the pub near mine? Then you won't have to drive.'

That's okay by me. I don't much like clubs, there's no

talking in films and the van will be safe enough locked up. Going to the pub is a thing that can be curtailed at will, when desire overcomes resistance. There's still the bottle of Champagne to surprise her with, so I'll try and time it all just right, 'Let's make a move then, shall we. I'll get the bill.'

'I'll pay half.'

'Not this time. What with all the travelling I've been doing I've landed a hefty bonus. Let the company pay for once.'

They say that your hearing is at its most sensitive at three in the morning. Is this because our ancient ancestors had to listen out for nocturnal predators? Is it still as sensitive if you are in the middle of a dream?

I lie awake at two forty-five, listening to the sounds of the night. The house is on a cul-de-sac. Without traffic the loudest sound is me rubbing my forehead, followed by the rise and fall of Dawn's recumbent breathing.

Two minutes ago I released myself from the enfolding embrace she always insists on after we have finished what she calls making love. I'm dog-tired, but something is keeping me awake. I know what it's likely to be, but I don't have to worry about that yet. Thinking all this stuff through is getting to be a pain.

The central heating went off hours ago, but the water is still making a noise in the radiator. There are two empty wineglasses on the bedside table and Dawn is lying beside me in quiet sleep. However much I try, I can't get to the truth of what I think about her. We've been doing this thing for coming on two years and I've enjoyed it for the most part. Dawn does the sex thing pretty much to my satisfaction and she seems to like what I do for her. We get along fine in those brief moments when we're together. She seems to think that I, John, am a good thing. She's even lied to the other John about what she was doing tonight to make sure the evening was going to be free. Still, when I look at her I can't see what it is she signifies. It's warm enough in here for me to lift the sheets up and look at her in her entirety, but I know that's not going to help. It's not the looking, it's the way of looking. I've been so close to this human being that there was nothing between us. Nothing between us. What happened to me? What are the insidious changes that occur when you're not on your guard? Why isn't there some mechanism for informing you that this sort of thing can happen?

In the morning I'll be gone. I'm probably not coming back. At some point I could have told you that. There were plenty of opportunities between the first rum and coke and the last glass of Champagne. Perhaps I should have tried harder to convince you to go away. The other John is perpetual bad news; it's up to you to break the cycle. If you said, at some point during the evening, that you were definitely going away, then perhaps I wouldn't be lying awake feeling that I haven't finished the job. I hate an unfinished job. An unfinished hem, with its dangling threads, never looks right. I can't let myself believe there are jobs that can't be finished, yet it may be that you're incapable of making that leap of the imagination. You have to realise that it only seems comfortable because it's familiar. Sometimes it's better to grasp the unknown and leave the rest behind, isn't it, John?

NORTH SHIELDS

It was steady out of Stockton. Roadworks had reduced a two-lane section to one and it took a long time to reach the A19. Some twat in a Vectra cut past even though the lane reduction was imminent. I passed the scattered cones later, then the remains of his nearside taillight, then himself, standing in heated discussion with the driver of a petrol tanker. I could see what was going to happen next, but sadly I would be too far past to enjoy it.

The A19 flyover, Billingham, the sprawl of processing plants and refractory stacks, smoke and steam billowing into the morning air. On the left the pillbox F1 hotel with its 'look at me' graphic. I stayed there once, before I met Dawn.

I definitely drank too much last night. My mouth is dry. Now that I think about it I never drank anything 'wet' the whole of the evening. I didn't even make tea this morning for fear of waking Dawn. I stood on the doorstep, half in, half out, wondering if I had my tactics right. If I said goodbye would she recognise the finality in my tone? Last night she was content in her Champagne haze; this morning she was quiet in sleep. I should leave without a word, be gone, and never go back. She can add John to the list of people who have let her down.

Dawn's doorstep: like the day half in and half out of the light. I could go back in now, before the latch clicks and I'm shut out. I could walk back upstairs and say, 'Look. I've got a load of money stashed away. Why don't we just get a flight right now and go east, like I said. Let's just go anywhere. When we get back we can sort something out. Sell the house, we'll move to another place. Don't think about the cons, everything's going to be fine.'

I could dump the van at the airport, forget about the rest of the trip and the consequences. Though I can't and it's odd, because John is capable of spontaneous action like that, more so than Ben, yet it's John who is going to drive back and face what's waiting for him. And that's why John can close the door and drive away as if the last two years count for nothing. In fact he has to: that's the sort of thing that John does.

The steel convolutions of the chemical works, the pillars of scaffolding are the playthings of giant demons, entrapping lost souls in clouds of acid gas, retorts for the production of sulphurous spirits. The air feels yellow, even if though it looks grey. Inside I can detect something of myself, forming or reforming at the base of my spine. I open the window in the hope that the damp of the morning will slake my thirst. Behind me the North York Moors are wind-lashed, but there's no doubting its appeal compared to my destination.

The traffic had cleared by the time I got to the sign for

County Durham. At Peterlee the sea and sky joined seamlessly far beyond the extent of the land. Another grey day, with a long way to go. Easington, Murton, Seaham: ex-pit settlements of an industrial revolution that has all but revolved.

Dawn would be awake now, up and fed and gone to work. What was this feeling? Guilt or dehydration? It's rare that you know you have seen someone for the last time. That only happens when you have visited someone you know is about to die. If you're not going again, then that's the last time. Simple. If then, you chose, unilaterally, never to see someone again, are you introducing something of death into the equation, killing off something of life? Let's not just say au revoir, let's say goodbye. Why am I thinking of Gail again, when there should be other things on my mind?

I've been trying to remember for some time where Gail-thinking came from. Since that first introduction, courtesy of Nick, I'd said hello to her a couple of times in passing. I started to notice her around college or, rather, I started to register that I was noticing her. But that's different from someone moving into the forefront of your thoughts. That's why I look for the moment and I choose a singular event to define this change of mind.

I'm aware that we reconstruct our own histories in simplified form. Each event is accompanied by a huge morass of detail that would be impossible to recall in all its complexity. So each memory must be synthesised from its core feeling or tone and enough detail to support the central idea. In many ways a significant experience operates on the level of fable, an object lesson or a moral question played out for real by a previous self. It can be a major point on the rising arc of the learning curve of life, but only if its message is made clear. All the extraneous detail has to be left in the still, leaving you with the pure spirit to consign to posterity. Pure spirit keeps a long time if it's looked after right. It's clear in the glass.

So I look for the shift into Gail-thinking and decide that it derives from the action of her dancing on the floor of the Student Union Bar, possibly to some washed-out contemporary soul thumper, probably to a four-four beat that kept her head moving in constant time to the music. I don't dance myself, but I don't mind watching, particularly if I have a drink in my hand and I can get away with not looking like a voyeur.

At that time Gail had long hair and each time she tossed her head it shook like a whiplash all the way down to the unsplit ends. With enough drink inside you this sort of thing can become mesmeric. If you can't find anything else to divert your attention, it can become all consuming.

There's always been something I've liked about the spectacle of effort: the pure, visceral pleasure of thought being put into motion. Better even than doing it is to see it, a symphony of muscular contraction and extension, rendered into heat and sweat.

I think we must have had some professional DJ for the

occasion, because each track segued seamlessly into the next. Gail kept dancing and I kept watching, thinking that, in a small way, I might like Gail to realise that she was being seen, at the same time hoping that I might continue to observe her unseen, enjoying the power of the concealed witness. Both hopes would seem to be incompatible but, in this sort of situation, where nothing is resolved and everything is to play for, you naturally aspire to the ultimate in every aspect of the game. I suppose, in the perfect world, you would have two selves: one who is cool and reserved and can keep himself together at all times and one who you can send out to make a fool of himself in a testing-the-water kind of way. Better still that you could have a rack of these extra selves to send out, one at a time, that could then be discarded once they had made an arse of themselves, leaving the cool one in some safe place marshalling the action.

I definitely know that the next track was *Enter Sandman*, because Gail had moved up a gear to keep up with the BPM. Her hair had become one ceaseless ferment of motion, catching the light and casting across her eyes like a fan at a Regency ball, creating allure out of the unseen. Sometimes the unseen, or the just seen, burns hot enough to brand its mark on the imagination. What is imagined to be seen, beyond anything actual or real, is then impossible to forget.

I'm not sure why I was sitting on my own in the SU, except that this might have been the occasion when my drinking buddies had gone off to town to see some thrash-metal band. Such things held little interest for me. Being that bit older made me feel like I'd done all that sort of thing better the first time around. So I was either being smug or stupid, because you're supposed to keep your mind open to new things to stop you getting old. In fact, it can often do you a world of good to make yourself do something that wouldn't normally be your first choice, just to make you sure that you don't end up being a collection of habits. Vanilla is never going to better rum and raisin but, if you invariably eat the latter, you end up with a mind like a funnel that can't adapt to life's little surprises when they pop out and surprise you. For these reasons I had ended up sitting on my own, with no one to talk to, sampling an SU disco that would normally be anathema to me, falling into the three-pint-an-hour rule that seems to come about when you haven't got anything else to do with your mouth. Worse still, my evening meal had consisted solely of one family pack of tortilla chips and I didn't really have the stomach lining to deal with that kind of alcoholic intake. What with the flashing lights and the spectacular combined efforts of all those heaving bodies, I was bound to be compromised defensively. That's what I say about the benefits of having an army of expendable selves: without a sacrificial *doppelganger* you end up expending yourself.

Gail wore a pair of flat shoes in a fetching shade of green. She had on an untucked shirt that was buttoned in only three places. I must have worn a look that said it all because, by the nub end of the evening I had been totally subsumed by Gail-thought. Whether that was because I had been working exclusively with men for the two years prior to going to college or whether I was dealing with powers beyond my control I don't know but, whatever I thought I had in mind, I was now going to get Gail-thinking instead. What I didn't know, though, was that Gail-thinking is so pervasive that it doesn't leave room for much else and that, however many years later, when you have more pressing things to think about, it will catch up with your white van on a cold road to the North.

They say the A19 is one of the most dangerous roads in the North East – all those people getting on for a short stretch, crossing, leaving, fucked-up on their way to work. I was finding it a drag – in and out of lane, making way for slip-road people too stupid to time it right, stamping on the brakes more than once to avoid a needless crisis. It was one of those days. You get them in cities and towns as well as on the road, days where everyone seems to have lost their sense of reason. People of all ages revert to some feral instinct or atavistic urge to hunt. A faraway look falls on their eyes and a simple trip to the shops becomes an essay in ways to survive. On the road it's a free-for-all. I put it down to sunspot activity, because I can't think of anything else.

Sunderland, steady going with sporadic spells of road

twats, window now closed because of the cold coming off the North Sea. Signposts to the Stadium of Light, giving the impression of a nineteen-sixties prediction of science fiction entertainment for the masses, visualising soma-induced trance show of laser beams and shifting polls of phosphorescence in the dark night. Perhaps the Mak'ems do see the light when Sunderland score at home. For me even the dim bulb of this sun is too much for tired eyes and I still don't need a piss – must be as dry as sand.

Dual carriageway, island, tailback, dragging on fumes from the bus in front. Somewhere the sun is shining, but not on Gateshead. Everyone is going into Newcastle today and everyone is using the A19 to do it. Queue for the Tyne Tunnel. *Time Tunnel*, I think. On the other side I'll come up in ancient Greece, but I'll be okay, because in this episode the ancient Greeks speak English. Come up instead on the northern border of the empire of ancient Rome and turn to follow the line of the wall into North Shields.

Cap and his mates weren't pleased to see me. Their eyes followed me as I turned in behind the club – eight eyes, eight legs – like a spider.

'You've taken your fucking time.'

'Traffic.'

'Traffic? There's no traffic.'

I had to admit, in the space of the club car park, their two cars and my van hardly constituted gridlock.

'You got the stuff?'

Melodrama: everyone thinks they are playing a part in some crappy film. 'Yeah, I've got your four in the back.' I may as well play my part in the scene, just to keep things even.

'Well, Johnny boy, that's not it, is it? We're expecting five.'

'Five?'

'Why aye, six.'

I was already out of the van, in the process of walking round to the back. Cap's friends were a touch too close for comfort. I knew Jackie, but not the other two. I could see they were all out of the same mould. A couple of times, early in the history of the trip, Cap and Jackie had taken me into the club for a drink. Cap had a key and opened up like he owned the place. I figured he was the doorman. Jackie would be an assistant doorman, or whatever you call them. Both times we passed an unpleasant hour while Cap inflated his ego and I looked at my watch, balancing my insistence that I had to be on the road with Cap's insistence that I stayed and drank another one. 'They're expecting me in Scotland,' I said, when in fact I was just popping up the road to a hotel I knew in Jesmond with secure parking. Then I was going for a Chinese buffet, an art film at the 'Tyneside' and an evening out on the town. I nearly copped it though, the second time. I was sitting in a crowded pub in the Bigg Market when Jackie came in and stood at the bar. Worse still, he was looking around for someone, so I had to duck down. I didn't think he or Cap would take kindly to a rejection of their hospitality, though I did toy with the idea of going up to him and saying that I'd been and come back, would he like a drink? Really, though, I didn't want to spend time with a bloke like that. In fact, I didn't want to spend time with a bloke of any sort.

Cap was breathing on me. Something told me he wasn't going to be asking me in for a drink today. He'd had more than enough anyway: I could have lit his breath. He smelled like he hadn't slept. Perhaps door duty gave way to drinking after hours.

'You're down for four. I'll get them out the back.' I didn't move.

'We'll take six. We ordered six, like.'

'You'll have to take it up with Terence. I'll leave four. Order up some more next time.'

He looked around at his mates in an 'I've got back-up' kind of way. 'Next time, he's saying.'

I think the script says that now everyone chuckles like bandits, before the ringleader turns poker-faced and reaches for his gun. Cap's mates made do with the dead stares.

'I'll unload your four,' I said.

'Ah, we'll take the four, then we'll take wor bit extra, on account.'

They were closing in on me. Cap alone was more than a match for me head on, unless I got him in the knackers, but that would take some conviction. In any case the others wouldn't put up with that. Now I was giving ground. I had the van key in my pocket. I could hold it in my hand so that the point stuck out between my knuckles. That would surprise him. I had to give up giving ground – bad strategy. Engage brain. I stopped, put my hand on Cap's chest and stopped him.

'Look, if I let you have more than four now I'll be short on the next drop. They won't like that.'

'Not my problem.'

'That's just it. The rest of the load goes to one drop in Glasgow. That's twenty odd boxes. If they're short of the sealing tape on one box they'll want to know what happened. When they find out they'll make sure it's your problem. The sort of outfit that can handle an amount like that don't like things to go any way, other than the way they say.'

I kept my hand on Cap's chest while he processed my lie. A good lie has an element of truth in it, they say. I guessed Cap was thinking about taking it all to another level and appropriating the lot. If so, he might have to consider that he was getting out of his league. I took my hand away to lower the ante.

'Give us the fucking four then, you bit shite.'

I stacked the four boxes on the tarmac. No one bothered to help. There were no goodbyes. I was gone. My mouth tasted of dust.

BORDERS

I was running late from North Shields. I would have liked to have stopped for a proper breakfast, but made do with a cup of tea and a bacon sandwich from a van parked in a lay-by. The day felt prematurely aged.

Much as I like Newcastle it was better to be out in open countryside. I brimmed the tank and set off up the A696, towards the A68, enjoying the fact that I was back on the road. The cacophony of thought, Dawn and Gail, Gail and Dawn, had given way to nothing, as if the next wave of thought was about to come along after the ebb of the last.

I'd been up the 68 before, but not to this drop. Mine not to reason why, but they wanted four boxes, which seemed like a lot for a new set-up. It got me thinking about Cap. The way he had looked back at his mates and the tone of his voice gave the impression that he knew something I didn't. Why did he think he could chance his arm for extra? He wasn't the buyer anyway, he was just the hired help. So what was behind the move? Not that you can ascribe much wit to these people, so perhaps it's simply food for my paranoia. But then, isn't paranoia like a lie? Doesn't it have to have a kernel of truth?

A tune on the radio was asking me if I knew the way to San Jose. No, but I knew the way to my second drop of the day. My boss is always exact with the directions, even though he had never been out to any of the drops. This new drop would be no different.

Terence is really the centre of gravity of the outfit. He looks like he's been carved from solid. When Dave first took me to meet him he was standing completely still behind a pile of shipping cartons in the corner of the workshop.

'Never call him Terry, or Tel or anything else. He don't like nothing but Terence, all right?' said Dave.

'What's he do if you get it wrong' I asked, purely out of academic interest.

'He'll get you wrong, you know what I mean?'

I wasn't sure I did, specifically, but the gist was plain enough. Terence was just standing there, stationary behind the packing crates, staring off a thousand yards. I wasn't sure whether he was deep in thought or just vacant. He was so unsettling that it was all I do to contain my reactions. Terence looked like an accident. I couldn't quite get it at first: he had big, stocky legs, like a rugby player, solid square hands that hung below square shoulders and that barrel-chest. It was his head! For such imposing bulk his head was tiny, like you were looking at him receding into the distance or had caught his reflection in a hall of mirrors. Quite bizarre.

He was making no obvious attempt to come back from wherever he had gone. Dave and I waited in patient, if awkward, silence. Finally he spoke, as if nothing had been amiss.

'What you got then, Dave?'

'This is John. He's going to do the riding for us.'

'Is that so?'

He held my hand in a loose grip and we shook, like making a deal. I felt like I'd signed a blank piece of paper.

'You like riding do you, John?'

'Yeah, I suppose. I've done enough of it'

'He's fuckin' pukka, aren't you, John? Been on despatch, the lot.'

I sometimes wondered whether Dave hadn't read instruction manuals on how to be a cockney geezer and taken it all rather too much to heart. Even the lock-up garage, with its wide array of boxes and stripped motor parts looked like it came straight out of an episode of *Minder*. Every now and then, though, he slipped out of character as if it was too much of an effort to keep up.

Terence raised his eyebrows, 'Despatch, yeah? And you're telling me he's reliable.'

I didn't read any irony into that. Dave was happy enough.

'You're straight, aren't you John?'

I had my own, ironic slant on how straight I was. Whatever was coming up was going to be a long way off the straight and narrow. That was obvious. Yet I was letting myself go along with it. In fact, I was already part of it, because I'd accepted Dave's money and even felt good about.

'Good, Dave, that's good.'

In all the time I've known him I've never heard Terence swear. He's quite softly spoken for a man who looks like he can deal with anything that's likely to come his way. You could be around him all day and you would hardly be aware that he was there. Now, of course, I know what he's capable of. He didn't even swear the time we were clearing out the last of the engine parts and he got his hand caught between the side of the tipper and the gearbox we were chucking out. I would have jumped over my own head, but he just shook his hand and carried on.

He kept mainly to himself. Dave seemed to do all the day-to-day running. It was Dave who came and went most of the time and it was Dave who paid me my money. 'Nothing like a handful of folding,' he would say, stuffing a bundle of notes into my hand. Dave was first point of contact if anyone came into the shop, but it was Terence who was doing the thinking. It was his idea to clear away all the engine stuff; within two days someone had come to take it away. He said something about the piles of out-of-date porn being dead weight, so whatever we couldn't sell ended up floating in the Thames (strangely enough I felt worse about this ecological vandalism than any of the more morally dubious stuff I found myself doing). Terence had a plan and everything went along with it. Dave would come back from one of his long conversations with Terence full of the joys of spring because they had the next step sorted out and there was going to be no putting it off. I was happy because the money kept on coming and there wasn't all that much to do for it. After the scam I didn't even have to turn up unless there was more clearing up to do or something needed to be taken out. The old bike got 'exchanged' for a new one which I could take home for personal use and was either legitimate or the next best thing. It was taxed and I rode it around freely, without getting stopped by the Police. It sat out on the street night after night without anything going amiss and I considered that, all in all, things could be worse.

The A68 is one of the best old-fashioned trunk roads in the country, following the rise and fall of the Cheviots, past the great mass of Kielder Forest and on to the Scottish border at Carter Bar, Rochester, Byrness, Catcleugh Reservoir. The river Rede flows below, in the valley, on a route the Romans took to garrison forts in the wilderness beyond Hadrian's wall. My wheels roll where hob-nailed sandals walked, on a surface deeper down in time. Northumberland is the least populated county in England. Here the farms are far out in the hills and the burns run with no one to see them but sheep. Dawn is getting more distant with every mile.

Northumberland looks like it has archaeology under every inch of its soil. I feel like I'm performing archaeology on myself. So much of it has lain undisturbed for so long that it's like looking at another civilisation. John's history is barely three years old; he remembers it all. Ben has been dead long enough for his stuff to have degenerated into myth and legend. Gail is in there somewhere, a rare find hinted at by slight anomalies in the topography.

Scotland – sixty miles an hour for the speed cameras, rethinking my notes to find the drop. What could they want with the stuff way out here?

The cloud grey had deepened and darkened the landscape in turn. The sky seemed lower; I was travelling in a thin world between firmament and terra firma. No doubt that soon water would transfer from one to the other. I wondered what sort of place I was going to.

It was a line of huge cinder-block barns roofed over in corrugated sheeting. I approached on a cracked concrete driveway bordered by piles of well-rotted manure and overblown with loose straw. I looked for a farmhouse, but there wasn't one. Neither was there anyone to meet me. There were no other vehicles. I drove past the line of barns to see if anyone was inside, but they were all padlocked shut. I checked the dash clock to confirm that I was on time and parked up to wait, watching for the impending rain.

With the engine turned off I could hear the forlorn bellowing of cattle in the nearest barn. It was echoed in the next one along; it reflected off images in my head while I waited for the rain. How long was I supposed to give it? There was a limit to how late I could be for my next drop. I had just arrived at the 'what ifs?' when a pick-up turned through the gate and parked up.

He was a young guy in a woolly hat and shit-splattered wellingtons. I wound the window down and he spoke, 'You him, then?'

'Yeah.' I must be, I thought, I'm not here for the milking, 'What about you?'

'I'm not him. He's coming soon. He wants you to wait in here.'

He started to walk off in a way that suggested he wanted me to follow. He may not have been the man, but he didn't appear malevolent. Nevertheless, I made him wait while I locked up the van. He took me past the lowing herds to the last barn in the row, shook the padlock in a way that opened it without the key and slid open one of the doors.

'In here,' he said.

'In there?'

'Aye, or you'll get wet.'

'Bit dark, isn't it?'

'There's light.'

'Is he going to be a long time, or shall I expect him, say, in ten minutes?'

'Aye.'

I took that to mean whatever it meant and entered the barn, keeping a weather eye on my back, just in case. My guide made as if to close the door behind me.

'You not staying?' I said.

'No.'

'Then you won't mind if I borrow this.' I reached around the door and took the padlock from its staple.

'Suit yourself.'

He shut the door anyway. I heard him clump off. His pick-up started and drove off into the distance. I slid the door back slightly to make sure he hadn't jammed the hasp in some way, then shut it again to keep out the draught.

There was a little light, as he said, though it took a while to get used to it the umbral haze filtering through the few translucent roof-lights. I could see objects forming in the dark.

In front of me was a stack of mattresses maybe eight feet high. Next to that a pile of clothes: dresses, trousers, a brown overcoat. There were two chairs upturned on a matching settee and a wooden dining suite doing a balancing act.

The rain had started. Fat northern raindrops were pattering on the skylights. The corrugations of the roof drummed in sympathy.

I could see more now. Stuff filled the barn. It formed rows down the length of the building with clear lanes in between. I walked down the nearest one, kicking up fine dust from the floor. There was an old set of golf clubs, a nineteen-forties veneer mantle clock, a cheap and awful painting of an alpine scene with a tear in the corner, a lonely drawer stuffed with correspondence, three wardrobes in a row, a Formica dining table, a gaggle of rusty garden forks, a Rotavator with no blades, a glass cabinet missing all its glass, a cane fishing rod, an ARP helmet, dozens of dried up pot plants.

I had reached the end of the barn. I turned and came up the next lane. There was all this stuff, old and dusty, not so old, but still dusty: a fibreglass bath, companion sets, an area given over to bureaux and desks. I could see piles of photographs: a colour shot of a village fete, or something, dated 1975, a graduation ceremony, some wedding snaps. Did men in the seventies always grow a beard to get married? A framed photograph stood on one of the desks: a nice couple in their fifties, taken in the fifties. A studio photograph. I bet they didn't own a camera. A wedding anniversary? I looked at them, he with his Brylcreamed parting, she with practised deportment learned at school. Was this their desk?

I looked around. It was a history of British interiors or, rather, the worst of a history of interiors: a standard lamp with a picture of a house on the shade, the type that allows light through a transparent patch where there is a window. How long has it been since I've seen one of those? What about a metal waste paper bin with scenes from the caves at Lascaux?

The door had slid open again. There was a man silhouetted in the gap. I walked over to meet him.

'Are you him,' I asked.

'Yes, you've brought it?'

'Yes.'

This man was older. His tone was soft and avuncular.

He didn't seem the sort to be one of our customers.

'Good,' he said, 'I have my vehicle outside. I hope I didn't keep you too long. We had a little trouble with a wall, but it's right now. Anyway, sorry for any inconvenience.'

'Not at all. If you don't mind me asking, what is all this stuff?'

'This stuff? Oh, we used to do house-clearance a few years back. Thought it would make up the shortfall. There were a few nice pieces one time or another, but you have to move a lot of stuff to find them.'

'Like panning for gold?'

'If you like. After a while you get tired of moving furniture about. Most of it's deceased estates. The relatives get the best of it, if knockers haven't beaten them to it. You get to tidy up the rest. It's usually more trouble than it's worth. You see that pile of suitcases?'

'Yes.'

'They're all leather. There's quite a good market for those. Every now and then I sell one of them, but most of the time it's not worth the bother.'

I followed him out into the rain. It was cold, but a change from the dry dust of the barn. My companion didn't seem to notice.

'I've backed up to your van. You do have it all?'

'Yes, four cases.'

I opened up the back and helped him load the boxes onto the tailgate of his Range Rover.

'They tell me this stuff sells itself, is that right?'

'I don't get involved at that end. I deliver enough of it. That's all I can say.'

'Ah well, anything's worth a try.'

We finished the transfer and I locked up the van. He was already walking back towards the barn.

I called after him. 'You'll find the padlock on the floor inside the door.'

'You off then? Well, thanks again.'

He hadn't thanked me a first time. Anyway, it made a pleasant change to be taken into account. In this business you don't see the best of people.

I got out of the rain as quickly as I could and started up. Luckily there was warmth enough left in the engine for the heater to blow hot straight away. I could still detect the stale scent of the storage barn, as if it had somehow attached itself to my clothes. It was the dry smell of lives that have passed away, the fetid odour of taxidermy and bell jars. I could see the picture of the anniversary couple and knew for certain that they were gone. I drove away.

The van was cold inside. Inside the barn it was still as death, while outside the rain was driven at an angle by the wind. I was at a loss. The barn had reminded me, in some way, of the unit. Right now, this far away, I didn't want to think about that. I didn't want to think about any of that stuff. The only way to do that would be to obliterate it with something else. At least for a while.

Pools of water were forming on the road surface. The pools hissed under the tyres as I passed. If it got any worse the van would become a submarine. I kept my eyes open and turned the heater up to dry out the puddle my boots had left on the floor. I gripped the wheel and tried to leave the barn behind.

THE BALCONY

My first, proper, going out date with Gail took place on a warm night in the spring of my last year at college. It was also Gail's last year, but she was in the year ahead of me because she'd been doing a four-year course. That was one of the reasons why our paths hadn't crossed too often in the time before. Now I'd found her and I was in the middle of trying to wind up my efforts towards the final push. I suppose Gail was doing the same.

Someone had turned up the brightness. It was getting hard to concentrate on all that stuff. The sun had come out early to help and, because it was warm, I was spending a Wednesday afternoon on the balcony outside the SU bar. By rights I should have been busy in the library but, for historical reasons, Wednesday afternoons were designated for sports and there was a longstanding tradition that, as there were no properly organised sports anymore, then pinball and afternoon beers were a worthy substitute. I'd played pinball for fifteen minutes to clear my head and then I'd decamped to the balcony with a book of critical essays and a pint of stout.

The balcony could only be accessed via a sash window in the function room. You had to carry your own seat through if you wanted to sit in comfort. In reality it wasn't even a proper seating area, but it had a south facing aspect and, in the unseasonable sunshine, it was just asking for it. Half a dozen other people had been thinking the same way, but luckily everyone was reading and no one was chatting. I settled in to my book.

The balcony was long and thin and looked out over the lawn and the road that lead up to the other half of the college. Being on the balcony made you feel like a bit of a rebel, over and above the people that were coming up the road to the SU and through the double doors below to get to the library and the buildings beyond. A lot of people came and went, but I didn't pay them much attention. I carried on working my way through the book right up until Gail appeared on the access road. I saw her straight away, heading across the grass towards the SU door.

She was wearing a light-coloured dress like one you might see on a statue of the Goddess Diana. Her legs were bare in the sunlight and she wore Doc Marten boots with contrasting laces. Her gait was smooth and unruffled, long steps, each foot placed straight in line with her stride. Her posture was upright, her face calm. She took no time to cross the grass. I had little time to decide on my course of action. On the one hand my conviction to carry on with my study, on the other my overwhelming desire to head her off in the SU foyer and make her time mine. But she was covering ground too fast, her attention focussed on the direction of travel.

For a moment a strange passion gripped me. I liked to

be cool, but I was gritting my teeth. The book was slipping between my knees. My mind had already slipped from my task and I was contemplating how I might launch myself back through the balcony window and pitch headlong down the SU stairs. I even considered dropping off the balcony itself to save time. It could only be ten or eleven feet and, if I let myself down with my hands… Then my window of opportunity had passed and I was left with only one real option. Gail would already be heading towards whatever she was doing and, if I went now, I would be chasing after her. At this stage of things that would never do. I fetched the book back up and tried to find my page, without success. Suddenly every page looked the same. Nevertheless, I wasn't going to be put off. If I could defeat my desire then I could get back the thread of what I was supposed to be doing. I found the right essay. I started from the beginning again, a conscious attempt to put the last couple of minutes out of my mind. Then Gail climbed through the window to the balcony.

'Hello Ben, what's new?'

How did she know I was up here? I'd watched her all the way from the road and she hadn't looked up once. I held out my book, 'Nothing new in any of this.'

She looked at the title. 'Other peoples' ideas,' she said.

'Want a drink?'

'No thanks, Ben.'

I began to feel a bit sheepish about drinking this early

in the afternoon, 'Soft drink?'

She leant against the balcony railing, one foot crossed over the other, framed by the sky. She looked to me a product of nature as much as the grass or the green trees of the campus. My feet were almost touching hers. We formed one continuous shape in my imagination. I filled the short distance between us with ideas. I tried to read the message in her eyes. I hoped that I filled her field of vision. I didn't want to look like a no-hoper drinking through the afternoon. She read me.

'Give me a sip of yours,' she said.

I passed her the glass and she drank an inch, slowly, as if it were as thick as milkshake.

'So what you doing?' I said.

'I'm off to see Ed Preston to discuss my project.'

'On a Wednesday afternoon?'

'It was the only time he had.'

'So you're just passing through?'

''Fraid so.'

I tried hard not to show my disappointment. Her dress was translucent in the sunlight. She was close enough to touch. She handed back the glass and I drank some myself, slowly, like forming a relationship, 'So, you going to be busy all afternoon?'

'Looks like it.'

'Pity, it's going to be a nice afternoon.'

'Yes, it's a pity, but a nice afternoon is often followed by a pleasant evening.'

We met at the crêperie just after eight. The dress had been substituted by a pair of black leggings and her green denim jacket. We had a table for two on the first floor, overlooking the street at the back of the building, far below because the land fell away there. It made you feel like you were perched high above everyday life. There was even a floor above the one we were on, but that was way up in the clouds.

'I don't think I've been in here since I first came to college,' I said.

'We used to come here quite a bit at one time.'

I didn't ask who the 'we' was. I didn't want to know. She handed me the menu. 'Hope you're not vegetarian, they don't do vegetarian all that well I don't think.'

'I'm not vegetarian. Would you like wine?' I hoped she didn't. It might make too much of a dent in my finances.

'No, I'll have a bottle of beer, whatever you're having.'

I hadn't said I was going to be having a bottle of beer. I was, of course, but I hadn't said it.

We ended up getting through a couple of bottles each. We had a main course and a dessert. I could fall asleep. I could stay in this moment with Gail for as long as it lasted. Sweet tension. If she felt it then she wasn't showing it. Always at ease. The night was dark outside, but that was another place. I was staying in this place.

She glanced at her watch, 'Home time.'

I looked at my watch, 'What, right now?'

'Come on, Ben'

'You sure?'

'Yes, I have to be back, busy day tomorrow.'

'I'll get the bill.'

We split the bill. She wasn't going to have it any other way. The crêperie had been warm. Outside it was cold

'Can I walk you home?'

She looked at me as if I was being a bit simple. 'You're coming back with me aren't you?'

The house was nothing like I'd expected. She'd told me over dinner that she shared a house with two other students, Bridget and Jane, so I was expecting the same sort of shabby, undecorated hovel that I had to put up with, along with my three washing-up-o-phobic housemates. My room was an oasis of calm amidst a flyblown dung-heap, but this was different: a proper home.

'This is nice. How did you find it?'

'It's Bridget's'

'What, she owns it? Is she independently wealthy or something?'

'Her parents bought it as a kind of investment. It gives her a place to live while she's doing her course and she gets to make some extra cash letting out the spare rooms.'

'Er, wow.'

We went through to the living room.

'Ben, Bridget, Bridget, Ben. Coffee?'

'Thanks.'

'Make yourself at home. Bee will keep you company. You want one Bee?'

'If you're making one Gee.'

'Jane here?'

'She's out with Foster.'

I sat on the settee. Bridget was in one of the armchairs, reading a magazine.

'I don't think we've met, have we, Bridget? I haven't seen you around college. Sorry, I haven't noticed... I mean...'

'No, I'm at the University.'

'Right, so how do you know Gail? She answer an ad or something?'

'I've known Gail since we were at school.'

'Oh, really,' I couldn't stop myself, 'what was she like at school?'

'Clever, a bit confident, pain in the arse...'

'I heard that.' A voice from the kitchen.

'...but ever so forgivable. A sweetheart, really'

'That's better.' Gail was back with the coffee already. She distributed them round and took hers to the other armchair. She looked towards me in a confidential way, 'You see Bee's never really forgiven me for being selected for the school volleyball team when she wasn't.'

'It was a fix,' said Bridget and they both laughed.

'This is a great house,' I said

'Thank you. It's not really finished, the décor.'

It looked finished to me. The three-piece suite we

were sitting on looked new. Beyond the living room was another room, a conservatory with stained glass panels, wicker chairs, a rubber plant, a wicker coffee table imported into this room on which I had placed my mug.

Such a long time since I'd been somewhere civilised.We talked about decorating for some time. Gail didn't say much. I got the impression that this might be Bridget's pet subject. I really only kept the conversation going to be polite, especially as this was Bridget's house and, on one level, I was her guest. With the food and the beer and the coffee I was getting to feel too comfortable and at some point I was going to have to get up and go and trudge my way back across town to my car and drive back to the hovel where, no doubt, the boys were busy working their way through the last, disastrous batch of home brew. Eventually I noticed that Gail had stopped making any contribution at all. She just sat, making a thousand sips out of her coffee whilst the two of us gabbed on about nothing. And then, without a word or any physical signal that I could detect, Bridget brought the conversation to an end, folded up her magazine, stood up and said, 'Goodnight.'

What?

Gail was still engrossed in her coffee. I put down my empty mug. I looked at the time on the mantelpiece clock, even though I was wearing my watch. I looked at Gail. She didn't say a word. I heard Bridget shutting the door upstairs. Gail put down her mug. I sat on the settee with my hands awkwardly at my sides, my mouth opened, ready to speak, but unable to get anything out, and, in the next moment she was kneeling on the settee, her legs astride mine, looking into my eyes, placing her hands on my shoulders.

'Now then, Ben,' she said and the distance between us was closed.

Sometime in the darkness of the morning I let her fall asleep. I wasn't going to sleep myself – not just yet. I'd heard Bridget use the bathroom and Jane come in through the front door. I'd been in Gail's bed for hours that had seemed like minutes. I had found a place where Ben's weary imagination had come to rest, where it was quiet and peaceful and felt like home and he had to enjoy it for just a moment more, before he went to sleep. Gail had a single bed, but it seemed to fit two. Gail and Ben were right and, in the dark hours, he was going to let that sink in before his head sank to the pillow and he had to make do with dreams.

TWEED

I made my way back down the A68 and turned up the 6091 to Melrose. The cold rain ran rivers down the windscreen. In the west the sky showed grey, promising lighter weather. I was trying to concentrate on keeping myself in the moment. The dash clock said that time was going fine, though time was going. I skirted Melrose and Galashiels, onto the A7, onto the A72. I picked up speed and drove upstream.

Clovenfords, Walkerburn, Innerleithen – to live and die in the valley of the Tweed. I could have brought Dawn here and disappeared. I have enough money to rent a place for a year, maybe more, probably more up here, such are the inequities of income and locale.

How easy is it to manufacture a new identity that functions on every level? A change of name and a change of address are simple enough, but what about a new National Insurance Number? There must be ways of doing it, because people do. There are so many lone houses here, on the banks of the river, looking down from the slopes of the valley sides. It's peaceful and, because it's different from the places I've been living recently, it seems like another world. It is another country after all, but there's no getting away from it, even if I wanted to.

After we cleared the space in the workshop the prophylactics arrived. There were lots of different colours, flavours and sizes, shapes for men and women, and tubes of spermicidal lubricant. My job was to open every box, take out the instruction leaflet and replace it with one written in Cyrillic script. It took forever.

'How are we going to sell these?' I asked Dave.

'We ain't selling nothing, this is trade,' he responded, with evident pride. 'This is your proper fuckin' trade.'

Two days after I'd finished, a big articulated wagon pulled up at the back and took the boxes away. In their place it left a hoard of rough wooden packing cases about five feet long and three feet square in section. Dave took a nail bar and cracked one open. It was full of long, thin woodshavings which parted to reveal... spades.

I picked one out and held it up to the light. The blade was a nice, sharp casting in pale, silvery metal. I thought it was stainless steel at first, but it was too light. The handle, though, was the flimsiest bit of stick you could imagine, rough, with no Y or T-piece handle, just straight, like an American shovel.

'These are a bit crap, aren't they Dave?'

'They're your fuckin' whatsit, your aircraft grade titanium alloy, ain't they.'

Apparently, these spades had come direct from the now defunct Russian aerospace industry. They had all this state–of–the–art materials technology and no funds for projects and expeditions. This was a way for thumb-twiddling scientists and middle-ranking bureaucrats to get paid, probably for the first time in months. Casting the material up as spades got them past military trade restrictions. They were never intended for B & Q, they were just money in another form. That's why the handles were useless, though the heads were probably unbreakable.

On the surface of it, Dave and Terence had got them in exchange for the prophylactics, but there was more to it then that. Dave gave me the impression that it was a fantastic bargain all round and I got a bonus to prove it.

There must have been plenty of money in it for them because, after they had off-loaded the bulk of the spades, we were out of the workshop and into our new premises within a week. To me it was just another anonymous business shed, but Dave and Terence were like pigs in shit. Evidently this had been planned for some time. Dave said they were now 'legit', though this had somewhat of a different definition to the one I was used to.

Not much came with us – just the paperwork and the last few items of aerospace gardening equipment. Any stuff we needed at the new place – furniture and fittings – was going to be bought in.

Cardrona Forest, Glentress, Peebles. I had lunch, as usual, in the Tatler Café, as usual, sausage, egg and chips. I was forcing myself to consider Dawn, because there was an injustice there. However much I tried, I still couldn't feel anything. I didn't feel happy about it, but I didn't feel particularly sad. Right now she would be at work; in a few weeks she would be expecting another call, but it would never come. In two or three months she might wonder how long it was going to be before I called. How long would it be before she knew that I was never going to?

Real people were eating in the café; real people were walking in the streets outside. Something happened to me that made me unreal. I'm sure I used to be real, I can remember being real, but I can't remember what it feels like. I have an inkling that it has something to do with making a connection with others. I've been on my own for a long time. That's why I don't feel anything with regards to Dawn. Even in her company I have managed to maintain my isolation. There may be advantages to that. It's difficult, for instance, for anyone to get under your skin and do damage. Yet there seems to be a trade-off – one to do with compromising some aspect of your humanity. In fact, I think I'm so far down that route that I wouldn't recognise those traits of humanity, even if I saw them.

I looked out of the window and watched the shopping people. *Everyone has their place and purpose. My only purpose is to do this job for the last time and face the consequences. I have no place. I have somewhere to live, but I have no place.*

'You drive a van?' Dave asked me.

I wondered what sort of van he meant. Were we going to borrow something big on a permanent basis?

'What do you mean Dave? A panel van or removal van or something?'

'Could be. You drive one of those?'

'Yeah, I suppose.'

'What about a map? You find yourself about all right? You know, north and that?'

'What Watford? Sure, despatch took me all over.'

'No, not fuckin' Watford. The other North, Leeds and Manchester, your whatsit? Newcastle'

'You tell me where, Dave, and I'll find it. What do you want?'

'We're moving into the delivery business.' That was Terence. I wasn't even aware he was in the room.

'Yeah, your proper fuckin' deliveries,' continued Dave.

'What we're asking, John, is whether you'd like to do a spot of work for us. It would take a day or two, every few weeks, easy work.'

'And what would I be delivering?'

'Something that's going to put this venture on the map.'

'There's no argument then, is there?'

'Thing is, John, there'd be a lot of capital tied up in the product. It would have to be looked after.'

'It wouldn't have to go astray, you know what I mean,' said Dave.

'Well you know me, gentlemen, Mr Reliable.'

They didn't honour that with a response. It wasn't that they were being threatening, just trying to emphasise the commitment.

'Does this mean I'm in line for a pay rise,' I asked, half-jokingly.

'Oh yeah,' said Dave, 'there's fuckin' money in it.'

I left the Tatler and drove out of Peebles on the 72. On the left, Neidpath Castle, once besieged by Cromwell. There is, apparently, nowhere that Cromwell did not go. He got himself around a bit, like me.

The rain had stopped, but the cold air still felt thick with the presence of water. White wisps of cloud were floating amongst the trees like ghosts, rolling into the glen along the line of the treetops. Traffic going my way was non-existent. I would like to tread lightly on the treetops. Perhaps I'll get my chance.

I'm riding up the river towards its source, though I will never get there: this road doesn't go that way. One winter, the Tweed suffered a drought, not because of lack of rain, but because the entire upper reaches, and the watershed beyond, froze solid. What did the fish think when the water stopped coming? What did the dry river look like?

From 72 to A721, westward bound with the failing sun in my eyes, across the top, observing the subtle changes in landscape from valley to fell: Elsrickle, Newbigging, Carnwath. Even the sun is cold and damp, unlike suns that shine on other worlds. This one is seen through successive panes of textured glass. Somewhere to the north is Braehead – the thought makes me shudder. Hell was cold to the Vikings. The only warmth I have here is enclosed in this small box of sheet metal. If I were to kill the engine this interior would soon chill.

The watershed slopes down towards habitation. Beyond the outlying villages and towns is Glasgow. You can feel its presence long before you get there. Between the field systems are golf courses and country clubs. Kilncadzow, Roadmeetings, Yieldshields, Carluke – I won't get to Glasgow.

Where do people like Terence and Dave come from? Doesn't everyone start their journey from the same point?

Dave I could almost understand: he was just a chancer with a limited intellect making the best of things in the only environment he knew. He wasn't likely to transcend his environment, because his destiny was restricted by his limited imagination. Making good meant making money and, as he wasn't going to be securing himself a remunerative job in the City, he had to find other means to find the means. Questions of morality didn't enter into it.

Terence was beyond me. He was as obviously at home in his environment as was Dave, but mentally he was in a different place. You could consider him a kind of intellectual pocket battleship: too fast to be caught by anyone that could outgun him, too heavily armed for anything that could catch him up.

I'd kind of got the measure of him before we left the old workshop. His eyes let you know. If he was approachable, they would be looking about, constantly sizing up the state of play. He would have a lark with Dave. They were close together in a way that made me feel they'd grown up that way. At other times he'd be staring off into the distance in that same way that he was when I'd first met him. Even Dave didn't bother him then.

They didn't have any friends that I knew of. They could both have been married and I wouldn't have known. No information was volunteered. I didn't volunteer anything about myself. I was never asked. In any case, people like these don't ask personal questions unless something about you is impinging on their universe. It suited me. Anyway, what was there to know? The circumstances of my existence had found a simplified form. We were just working geezers – we operated on a business footing.

Nevertheless, I was still the outsider. There was definitely a worker/management thing going on, even without the factory time clock and PAYE

I saw the stuff for the first time one day after I'd come back from a last-minute delivery job. There were buckets of it – literally. There were forty or fifty paper-bin-sized buckets with snap-on lids. Each was full to the brim with resealable plastic bags full of the stuff. Dave had some of them open on his desk and was weighing the contents on a set of scales. He looked like a man whose just been told about his new-born and it's going to be fat cigars all round. He saw me come in and said, 'Nice', but he was talking to himself.

'Well then, John, you got nothing on for the afternoon?'

'Nope.'

'Get hold of the tape gun, will you, there's a load of cartons to make up.'

Terence was unloading the cartons from the boot of his car, bundles of ten held together with nylon binding tape. I went to fetch the Stanley knife but, by the time I'd got back Terence had snapped the binding by hand. I didn't think such a thing was possible.

We passed a more or less pleasant afternoon measuring and packing the stuff into plastic canisters and then into the made-up cartons. The plastic canisters were plain grey, the cartons unlabelled. I got to thinking how prosaic it all was, compared to our product's potential, how down-to-earth all this preparation for shipping. I could have been boxing up party hats or novelty pencil rubbers. I knew as soon as I'd seen the buckets what the main thrust of our business was going to be about. This had always been the intention, right from the phone scam, and here I was mucking in without drawing breath. But then, I didn't think about it too hard on that afternoon and I never have.

At the end we had twelve cartons stacked by the shutter door. Dave looked really pleased. Even Terence looked pleased, in his own way.

'Time for a drink,' said Dave.

'Yes,' said Terence.

I was about to agree when Terence said, 'Tomorrow at ten, John. Bring a change of clothes, you'll be driving.'

I went off for a drink by myself

The van was parked outside the shutter door when I arrived in the morning. It looked clean enough, not brand new, but not an old nail. Dave came out and tossed me the keys.

'Take a look,' he said.

It was pretty clean inside as well. The load surface was a bit scratched, but not like it had been transporting anything heavy duty. The engine started okay, clattered to life like most diesels, but it didn't sound like it had driven to the moon and back. I ignored the odometer – the numbers were out of line.

When I'd finished I noticed Terence standing by the shutter door. He'd probably been watching me the whole time. He had a habit of doing it, especially if you were on with some aspect of his business – not that that made it any less unsettling. I got up and walked past him into Dave's office.

'All right?' said Dave.

'Seems all right – won't really know about the running gear until I've taken it out on the road.'

'There won't be no problems.'

I guessed they weren't going to be short-changed on a

vehicle.

'I take it I'm going out on a delivery.'

'Yeah.'

'Where to, then?'

'Daventry...'

No problem.

'...some place in Derbyshire, Sheffield, Doncaster, Middlesbrough, Newcastle...'

He was reading them off a list. He looked up at me and clocked my expression, 'Problem?'

I don't suppose there would have been any point discussing British topography with him. I'm sure the map in his head showed London the size of Germany with the rest of England a tiny Denmark perched on the top. Scotland probably didn't figure at all: just an idea from a shortbread tin.

It started as simply as that. Terence had the precise instructions, but I don't think even he had fully grasped the reality of the journey times. I got it all done, but I wasn't back at the unit until the early hours of the morning. The same day I had to go to the Northwest on another run. That didn't take as long though, by the time I got back, you could have sponged me off the driver's seat.

Whether it was because I was tired or because I wanted to have a little control over my destiny I don't know, but as soon as I was back I said straight off to Dave, 'Why don't I devise a route?'

'A route?'

'I'm assuming here that there are going to be more trips to come.'

Two months later I was out again. We were in business. This time I stayed over in Newcastle and did the Northwest bits the next day.

From the start the contents of each carton was standardised. Each deal was set on the number of cartons; the cost to each customer for a carton was the same. There were no bulk discounts, because even one carton could be considered bulk. In any case, no customer knew the details of another. All they had to know was that no one else was being supplied in their area. I heard Dave asking if that was wise, considering that we might be able to offload a whole lot more in a big city, but Terence said it was right – it was the repeat business that would reap the rewards. It didn't do to upset the customer.

I don't know what network Terence used, whether he met the customers, or whether it was done entirely by phone and e-mail from the start. I don't know what method of payment was used. I never saw any money changing hands. For all I know Terence sent out proper invoices with thirty-day payment terms. My money kept coming. Dave and Terence bought new cars and started to look like they were acquiring wealth. We had a covering business shifting ex-rental videotapes, but there must have been peanuts to be made from that.

Customers came and went. Some stayed the same. Orders went up. Orders went down. The general trend was up. Eventually the delivery route expanded to three days. The money kept coming in.

John let it all go to his head. He drank a lot of fine wine and hung around in upmarket venues trying to attract women of the upwardly mobile persuasion. He met with limited success. Perhaps they could detect the smell of bike oil on him: such things don't wash off too easily. He spent some time gambling, until he came across a book that outlined the statistical chances of winning. After a while he settled on a life of eating out or ordering in and spending his time alone. There were no longer any connections with the life of Ben. He had left no forwarding address. He never went to any of the places that Ben used to frequent. Any photographs that he had were closed up in a shoebox and shoved in the back of a cupboard, behind a pile of things that were awkward to get out. Any old letters were disposed of in a ceremony of incineration. When he looked at them they were written to someone else anyway. It was easy. All of Ben's worn out old clothes went in the bin, even his old leathers, which had his shape impressed in them. If he got sick of being at home he got his bike out and rode around, sometimes too fast. Every month or so he got to see Dawn and relieve the sexual tension. In the meantime, the white Astra van that the boys had got him stayed up at the unit and he kept his answer phone switched on in case he was needed.

Where do people like me come from? You can't look at yourself from the outside to get a picture and, if you're occupied on something that might have repercussions for your soul, then it's best not to spend too much time looking around on the inside. Best to make sure that you keep travelling forward and concentrate on staying on the road.

MOTHERWELL

.

Wishaw, down past the high-rise blocks into Motherwell. It was long enough since dinner to be feeling my mid-afternoon torpor. This far north it is dark before four this time of year. The streetlights glowed a boiled-sweet red, more pleasant than the sodium glare to follow.

I made a few, familiar turns and came to a stop just inside the factory gates. It was a long time since the place had actually made anything, it was now more of a warehouse.

Mabel came out. Mabel is a man – a man who moves boxes for a living. I threw him the keys to the van: here there were no problems with security.

'How are you, John?'

'Fine Mabe, not too late I hope?'

'We've not knocked off yet.'

Yes, the employee parking spaces were all still full, 'I forget how the other half live sometimes, pissing about in a van all the time.'

'No problem.'

I understood that, the company was busy. Motherwell was a different place to the old steel town. There are people that like to work. Mabel is one of those people.

I watched him unload the six cartons. He never let me help. This was his bit of responsibility.

'That'll do it,' he said, 'Bill wants to see you.'

'He does? What about?'

'I don't know. He just said I wasn't to let you go until he'd seen you.'

'Where is he?'

'In his office.'

I made my way between the stacks of boxes in the warehouse, boxes full of condoms and lubricating gel and other sexual accessories. A lad in bib and brace acknowledged me as I passed. A girl with ample breasts leered at me from the December page of the calendar. I found the stairs and went up to Bill's office.

He looked up from behind his desk, 'Ah John, how are you?'

'Fine, Bill, fine...'

I once got stuck here. There was snow in the East, making swift progress impossible. The snow had stopped by the time I reached Wishaw, but was replaced by thick fog. I was already hours late. By rights Bill could have been pissed off, but he was more concerned that the journey had caused me trouble. Even Mabel had waited. Bill got on the phone to Terence and smoothed out the problems about missing the next drop.

'Tell them you can't see your nose in front of your face up here, nothing's moving.'

I asked him where the nearest hotel was, but he wasn't having any of it.

'You'll come home with me,' he said.

So I spent the night at Bill's house. I ate dinner with him and his wife Justine and their daughter and he told me how he had got started converting old Beech Nut chewing gum machines to sell condoms in pub toilets. Retail led to wholesale and greater things. He had supplied the stuff we sent to Russia.

After dinner he took me out and got me drunk and wouldn't let me pay for a drink. I remember making slurred jokes about the Flowerpot Men, until it finally occurred to me that he knew me only as John. In the morning he brought me a cup of tea and wished me a safe journey...

'Mabe said you wanted to see me about something.'

'Nothing important. It's a bit cold. Thought you might want to take a warm up here. Sit down a while.'

I looked at my watch.

'You've plenty of time, if your next delivery's the same.'

'It's the same.'

'Just five minutes, you'll miss the rush, still.'

He was probably right, but it wouldn't do to be too late getting to the M74. I sat down.

He remained silent for a while.

'Something wrong, Bill?'

'What? No...would you like a spot of LeapFrog?'

Odd, he had never offered me a drink at the office before. Without waiting for my reply he brought out a bottle of Laphroaig and a couple of glasses. He poured a full glass.

'Not so much for me Bill, I'm driving.'

We drank together, not saying anything. He finished his quickly and poured out another.

'Business good, then, John?'

'Seems to be. It's certainly regular. You must shift enough.'

'Oh aye, there's no shortage of demand. Never seems to be a shortage of cash to buy it either. You have to give Terence his due, he knows his market.'

'Yes.'

'Really, he doesn't miss much. You can't fault him on his attention to detail.'

'No.'

He went quiet again. I sipped at my whisky. It tasted of smoked peat and ancient history. Bill knew something, but he couldn't tell me. I had a good idea what he knew. I might even know more than he knew. Sometimes I think that, if everyone told everyone else what they knew, then most of the world's problems would go away, just like that. Then we could start all over again, with open government and transparency in all things. I'm all for it. Bill can keep his secret, though. I like him and I don't want him to feel bad on my account.

'Tell you what Bill, I wouldn't mind another.'

He filled it up this time. It seemed to make him feel better.

'How are Justine and the kids?'

'Oh, they're fine. Lauren's gone up a school now.'

'She'll knock them dead up there.'

'Aye, they get older, they get interested in other things.'

'Too true. Like all of us eh?'

'Maybe. I think I like things to stay the same sometimes.'

'Some things, for sure.'

The office was getting darker. Bill made no move towards turning on any lights. We sat there, looking at each other in washed-out colour. He still didn't speak. There is something to regret. That is all. I drank my whisky. Time to go.

'No worries, eh Bill?'

'No worries, John.'

I got up. He got up and reached over, shook my hand, held on longer than was strictly necessary. I could feel the whisky taking effect.

I took a few short breaths before starting the van. I left the window open as I drove off, listening to the hiss of the traffic on the wet streets as I tried to beat the rush hour. It was too early to be drinking. The middle day is a long day. At the end of this middle day I had somewhere new to find. There were many miles to be travelled in between.

Bill and Terence had known each other before the deliveries started. Bill acted as Terence's representative north of the border. Bill might know about the stuff that had been going on recently. He may not have seen the things I had seen, but he would have an idea what the plans were. The thought of it made me miss the traffic light going green. How unprofessional.

This is as far north as I go. It's like reaching the top of the roller coaster – slow through Motherwell then fast down the M74 on the other side. It's also the halfway point for me. In twenty-four hours I'll be back. Just twenty-four hours, give or take. It doesn't seem long. If you want to make time last go on a journey. Look back at incidents on the journey – moving on makes them seem remote. For me, waking up in Dawn's bed this morning was half a lifetime ago.

I rode down the M74 in the dark. I'm always amazed how dark it is. Away from the motorway the mountains are masses of immense black with barely pinpricks of light to show human habitation. The effect goes on for miles. Each light is a tiny ship amongst giant waves. There is only the rumble of your own little ship and the ships that travel with you, on the trade route. All else is nothing but the unknown sea.

I kept to eighty, trying to keep ahead of the rush, then remembered the whisky and slowed down. It wouldn't do to be stopped now. I needed something to soak it up, something to eat, a cup of tea? Where are the next services?

M6

Gretna Green, Carlisle, back into England. Steady at seventy making time with the wagons. Somewhere south the dome of Lakeland rises into a wet sky. On the fell tops the wind must be fierce, but here, between the rise to the west and the Pennines in the east the air is relatively still. Driving has become automatic; it's simply a matter of eating the distance.

There was still plenty of traffic; there always seems to be traffic on the M6. If it had been summer, and I'd had more time, I might have taken the old A6 and taken in the scenery, even at the risk of getting caught up behind slow-moving vehicles. Then again, I'd seen it all before.

I turned on the radio and listened to some classical for a while. Any other time it might have worked, but this time I couldn't be bothered to engage. I switched over to hear Chuck Berry chuntering briefly about a car ride and took in three tracks from the seventies that told of a west coast far different to the one where I was travelling.

In heavy goods there are two categories: trunkers and trampers. The trunkers do the regular work, picking up a load, carting it along a route, dropping at a destination. There's a finite job to do; they get it done, with possible allowances for the state of British roads. Much of the stuff that was accompanying me down the M6 was composed of trunkers.

Then there are your trampers. A tramper might get a call to pick up a load of remoulds from Leeds and take them Bristol. He'll be told to stop off in Gloucester on the way and collect two pallets of ceramics. On the way into Bristol he'll be told to drop and get back on to Birmingham for three pallets of premium beer. From there he might go back up to Leeds and make up his load with machine parts. Then he's off to Lille with the ceramics. From Lille he's bound for Cologne, stopping off in the outskirts of Paris for six reproduction Rodin statues destined for Copenhagen. He gets stranded in France for two days, because there's no goods traffic permitted during part of 'le weekend'. And so it goes on. After two weeks he gets to put his feet up at home for twenty-four hours before getting a call to go again. I think I would like that. Maybe not the punishment of being in the cab for the long hours, but certainly the unpredictability. Human beings are designed to adapt to events. I like to adapt to new stuff, but I suppose there are limits.

The new premises were a nondescript industrial unit between Heathrow and West Drayton, where we could hear the flights roaring out at all times of day and night. Dave liked that – I suppose it reminded him of 'your proper fucking trade'. On the surface it looked like we might be exposing our operation to the scrutiny of our neighbours, but really there was nothing to see. Every so often, when a trip was coming up, I went down and helped Dave pack up the stuff, ready for shipment. A couple of days after I'd be sent out to deliver it. Not a particularly hectic lifestyle, but certainly a rewarding one. The route started out at two days, but soon got rationalised to three. Early on there were fifteen or so cartons, but soon there were nearer thirty. Business was good and Terence and Dave bought in nearly new, matching S-Class Mercedes. I got another pay-rise and I started putting a bit of money away.

I forgot all about Ben and took to being John all the time. John was cool. He had no problems because there were no connections. He wasn't emotionally attached to anyone, so there was no comeback. He was never really lonely, in his flat, because he was new to himself. Anything that had happened was down to fickle twists of fate or destiny or something like that. If he got bored he got on his bike and ripped around for a while. Sometimes there would be a package to take out and he would rip around for money. All in all, it was just fine.

Penrith, Tebay – no time to stop at the services. To the east the A685 is laid on the path of the old railway. You can travel at speed up the valley of the Lune, along straight runs and sweeping curves that seem somehow out of place. Perhaps all roads would be like this if they hadn't been superimposed on the old cart tracks meandering along the field boundaries. What would the waggoners have made of the Scammel I've just passed hauling nigh on sixty tons of Challenger II? Everything's got out of scale. It's like the modernist nightmare of people dwarfed by giant machines, though all so often it's the compass of the juggernaut processes of multi-national business and national government that make you seem small. If I'm going to feel small, I would prefer to judge myself by the scale of mountains and the force of the tide.

I checked the time. The journey was dragging. There was still a drop to go. Then I had the other thing. My bag was in the back to try and cool the wine, but it would still be too warm. Perhaps there'd be ice. Ice was falling now – one or two flakes of snow – then none, as if nature were testing the nerve of we drivers, just to say, 'Look what I can do, if I feel I want to.'

Kendal, Carnforth, Lancaster, now feeling the wind coming off the sea. There's a way between the junctions, but soon they'll be stacked close together as I reach the conurbations of the Northwest. Garstang, Preston, Blackburn, Leyland. Chorley, Adlington, Standish, sick of the fucking motorway and the cut and thrust of the masses of traffic moving between the cities and towns. Wigan.

There are twos and threes in this business. It's an activity that takes place right at the edge of things. Few people are involved. In the end, of course, it affects many but, at the supply end of things, it's a small community. You get to trust half a dozen people at most. Everyone else is to be distrusted as a matter of course.

When I think about it I can count the number of people I can trust on the fingers of one finger, but it's getting to the point where I'm not that sure I can trust myself. I can't even get my own name right.

Terence looked at me strangely. He never looks at you right, but it was a different strange. Dave was as always: ebullient, friendly, prone to mockney mannerisms and ready with the cash. Still, I know for certain that this is my last trip. Specca told me that, wordlessly, the way he looked at me the last time we met. Terence told me the same, from his side, without words. So much is said when it isn't. Then, when I left for this last trip, I saw that there were cartons made up that I wasn't taking. I've always taken all the cartons, so what does that tell me?

It was going-out time in Wigan and I was still at work. On any other occasion I would have completed the drop and gone to one of my regular hotels, but not tonight.

I tracked down by the old engineering works, through the town, followed the signs for the Pier for two turns. No matter how many times I had done this route I always struggled to maintain my sense of direction. There must be some magnetic anomaly in Wigan.

I found the estate – just a normal, suburban estate like the one I had left that very morning – and passed two side roads, took a third and made my way down a cul-de-sac to the end house. I double-parked – there were already four cars parked outside.

The guy opened the front door

'You're late,' he said.

'Better late than never.'

'You say.'

'Where do you want it?'

'Bring it in here.'

I knew from experience that he wasn't going to help. I took a box, then had to move the van to let someone out – a woman who looked older than she dressed. After the second someone came and blocked me in, but he came and went before I'd taken the third. He kept his face away from me all the time, like I was the press at a high-profile court case.

'That's it.'

'Wait,' the guy said.

I waited inside the hall while he checked the contents of one of the boxes. It took a long time – time enough for me to get the gist of a football match playing on the telly in the next room, I could tell there were three of them in there, I could tell which team they were backing.

My guy in the hall lost count and had to start from the beginning. I'd seen him every time I'd dropped here, but on no occasion had we had what you'd call a proper conversation. I wanted to suggest he keep a tally with a five-bar gate or some such but it was far too late in the day to make a precedent like that. I waited until he had nearly reached the end again and said, 'It'll all be there.'

'You say,' he replied.

I was just taking the piss really. I knew he would have to start again. None of the customers had ever been short-changed on a shipment; I would never have worked for an outfit that operated like that. I knew I would have to wait in the hall until he had counted to a conclusion, so in a way it was a bit of an own goal, but I was willing to pay the price if it meant I could get him back for his lack of manners.

He took the finished case and placed it on an old set of shop scales sitting incongruously on a table in the open space underneath the stairs. I could see him mouthing the given figure to himself by way of remembering. Then he weighed the other two cases and mouthed their figures back to himself to see if they tallied. Of course they were going to, all three cases were the same, each had the same contents. Anyway, he seemed satisfied, though for all he knew the other two cases might have been filled with an equivalent mass of sand, or whatever. But who was I to interfere with his flow of logic?

He made me wait while he took the boxes upstairs. I could hear a girl's voice, but not what it said. He came back down.

'You can go now,' he said.

'Why thank you,' I said, with as much mock-enthusiasm as I could muster. Whether it registered I couldn't tell: I was already out of the door and he had shut it behind me.

I wanted, more than anything, to have finished driving for the day. There was too much traffic, too many people going out, too many people on the M6, too many cones between J22 and J21 with nothing, it seemed, to be coning-off for. At least I was stationary long enough to recheck the address and revise my route on the map. I looked up to sky, but it was blanked out by the glare of the streetlights.

THE MAUVE DRESS

I only realised how I felt about Gail on a Saturday in early May, during that last term at college. Both of us had been desperately trying to catch up on our coursework. We had agreed not to see each other between the Sunday night and Saturday morning, to treat the intervening week as a working week because we were getting so far behind. In truth Gail was trying to help me out. She seemed to be on top of her work all the time. I bet she'd been like that at school, coming straight in and doing her homework so that she had the rest of the evening free to do what she wanted. I'd always watched telly and put off my homework until the very last moment, even though I lived in a state of constant stress because of it.

We hadn't spent as much as five days apart for months, only over Easter, when she'd gone home to her parents and I'd been trying to make ends meet working in a fish-packing factory, the sole advantage of which was the opportunity to overdose on king prawns. The money stank almost as much as I did at the end of the day. The experience was too much like my pre-college days, taking what I could get, and I didn't like it. Somehow, with my eight ninths of a degree, I was now above that kind of thing. I tried not to think about Gail, just that I had been sent for a purgatorial refresher course, that it was finite, that I would be allowed back and that everything would be okay again. Knowing that meant that I could suffer things not being okay because they were going to come to a stop, if not soon enough. I spent my time incommunicado. None of my friends had stayed about, because they had family commitments or whatever. Gail had gone with her folks to France, where her mother's sister lived. She had told me where that was, but I didn't really take it in. I preferred to think that she had gone somewhere unreachable and that was that.

Since the beginning of term we'd more or less been in each other's pockets. She was off doing teaching practice much of the day and I had to spend lots of time trawling through an endless list of set texts but, nevertheless, we met up at least once a day and, every night I could, I went round to her place at Bridget's and made room for myself, with her, on her single bed, folded in the glow of the central heating and listening to Bridget filling and emptying the bath and cooking her hair with a hair dryer. Therefore, it was a considerable effort of willpower to agree to concentrate on work for a week and keep apart. The only way it could be done was if we had a definite time and place to meet on Saturday. The place had to be on neutral ground, away from our study materials and interference from any of our friends and the time had to be cast in stone.

'Why don't we meet at The Tea Shoppe?' she said.

'The Tea Shoppe? When have we ever been to a tea shop?'

'Sometimes it's nice to have tea and cake in the morning.'

'Isn't it even nicer to have a big cooked breakfast?'

'Come on Ben, I feel like being civilised for once.'

Perhaps she'd got used to being civilised over in France. It didn't matter to me. If she'd asked to meet me on the moon I would have gone.

'Ten o'clock, then?'

'Yes, ten,' I said.

In the event I was late. I'd fallen asleep in one of the armchairs at home, working my way through *Richard the Third* for the third time, and woken up in a panic, not knowing where I was. Then I'd found my bed and slept until it was broad daylight and there was no way I could get to Gail on time.

When I got to the tea shop she wasn't there. I had managed to be just twenty minutes late. She could have waited. She wouldn't have been late herself. I knew that, but twenty minutes was no time to wait, even if you're having to sit on your own with five days of anticipation built up inside of you. Nevertheless, I'd cast my eyes over the assembled throng and she wasn't there.

'Ben!'

She was there, only it wasn't her. Her hair was tightly curled into ringlets. I'd been expecting her green denim jacket, but she was wearing a jersey dress in pale mauve. Her legs were in cream tights or stockings with little flat shoes. She was wearing lipstick, the only time I'd ever seen her with it on, and she smelled different to her normal self.

'Quickly, take a seat.'

She didn't seem irritated. I couldn't quite equate her with the Gail I knew. I thought I'd seen her entire wardrobe, even in the few months I'd known her.

'I'm sorry, I had to order.'

'It's alright.'

She had the remains of a pastry and the last dregs of a black coffee. She usually liked a cappuccino. I thought about the froth and her glossed lips. I was going to say I was sorry for being late, only I couldn't stop looking at her: how the dress fitted her shape as if it had been made with her in mind, how the 'V' of the neck came down far enough to show the soft ridge of her collar bone without being low enough to reveal her cleavage. With her curled hair she looked softened, like it was impossible to get a proper focus on her.

'I'm...' I said. Then said nothing. She wanted to speak.

'I'm sorry, Ben, but I have to go in a minute. I'd completely forgotten that I have to go to a wedding.'

'Wedding?'

'It's my cousin, Jane. I have to go in a few minutes, Bridget's giving me a lift.'

'...' I meant to ask where it was, but that didn't seem to matter. It was somewhere else.

'Do you mind?' She smiled slightly.

'No, of course I don't. You should have a good time.'
'Sorry, Ben.'

'I, er, will you be back later?'

'There's an evening do. I don't think I'll be back 'til late.'

'No.'

The waitress had arrived, 'What can I get you?'

'Er, I don't know... tea. Thanks.' *Wake up, Ben, get a grip.*

Gail picked up the pastry and broke a piece off. It passed her lips without leaving a fragment. She lifted her coffee cup and drank the last little bit. She was like nothing I'd ever seen before, only heard about, or imagined, in some other time or place. I felt like a rough animal that had managed to sneak indoors for a few moments, but was soon going to be found out.

She looked at her watch: a small white disc on a blue leather band. 'Ben, I have to go. Bridget's waiting in the car park. I'll catch you tomorrow.'

She stood up. 'Right.' Then she bent down and her lips brushed against the stubble on my cheek, the lightest touch – too light to leave a trace of lipstick behind.

She reached beneath the table and picked up a small blue handbag that I also didn't know she had. She went to open it.

'I'll get this,' I said.

'Don't be silly,' she said and brought out a five pound note, straightened it and put it on the table.

It stayed there after she'd gone, like the image of her walking to the door with her pale legs and the mauve dress. I was lost at sea, in a stupid way for an everyday Saturday. My tea arrived and I drank it in an instant, realising that I hadn't had a drink for something like sixteen hours. I picked up the last bit of her pastry and it exploded into crumbs. The five pounds was far too much for the bill. I wondered why Bridget was taking her and why she hadn't asked me for a lift. I wondered where her cousin lived. It couldn't be too far if she was going to be able to get to a wedding for the normal sort of time. Was Bridget invited? Was she going to hang around for the day? Would someone else be bringing her back? I wanted her back. There was a void in her exact shape on the seat beside me. I felt sheepish about pocketing the change from the five pounds. I left a tip and put the remainder in a different pocket from my own money. I went out of the tea shop looking for something to do that completely occupied one's mind.

WILL

M56, heading west, trailing a white Merc Sprinter at eighty. I suppose, if the job had a future and business kept on expanding, I would end up in one of these. Maybe we could sign-write the sides with 'T&D Enterprises', or something similar, and lose the anonymity. But, then, anonymity's what it's all about.

I had the radio on to keep me going. I was so tired. It would have been nice to hear one of Gigi's traffic reports – images of what's happening on the road network make you feel that you're locked into some immense interrelated system of flux and intent. At all times mass is in motion to different destinations, altering the balance of the world like tides. It's sometimes nice to imagine that there are other fools like you, out there, trying to get the job done despite their road-weariness.

The engine needed a rest. I don't know why but, if you keep on going, an engine sort of loses its edge. Perhaps the oil gets too thin or hotspots develop in the cylinders or it just gets bloody-minded, but half an hour's rest usually gets it responsive again.

I needed more than half an hour. I was driving automatically through a cold evening with the smell of the Irish Sea. To my left, Delamere Forest, to my right the broad sweep of the Mersey.

So much of our culture revolves around these river courses; the very siting of our towns and cities is a result of their geography. Where there was no suitable watercourse they made one – somewhere over there is the Manchester Ship Canal.

You would think, with all this tele-working and the decline of shipping and heavy industry, that these cities and towns would gradually dissipate to the countryside, but if anything the reverse is true; right now I can see the lights of Liverpool across the water and Birkenhead ahead of me.

The Sprinter left the motorway and, for a while, I was left alone. I took heed of a whim and moved over to the middle lane for a spell, imagining that I was the last man left alive and that the amber glow in the distance was radioactive aftermath to which I was immune. The thought came as a strange comfort, but the spell was soon broken by an XKR doing about one-ten which passed me in the outside lane. I hadn't even seen it coming. I tried to catch it up – no chance.

M53, A55, A41, skirting close to Chester, placed commandingly at the extent of the navigable Dee. I had the rest of the directions in my head. I followed them: a few turns, a line of trees, a half-timbered house set in its own grounds with two sculpted yews at the garden gate. At the side a double garage with half-timbered effect and standing for three or four cars.

I turned off the engine and sat for a moment. The

engine sighed and so did I. My breath felt strained, as if I'd been holding it for too long. I tried to breathe through my nose until it settled. Then I reached into my bag, collected the bottle of wine and headed for the front door.

We just stood in the hall, looking at each other. He looked pretty much the same, only with a bit more weight on his shoulders.

'How are you doing?' I said.

'Fine. We're all doing fine.'

'Good...how's the job going?'

'I changed jobs two years ago.'

'Did you? More pay?'

'Better salary, better prospects.'

'Good. Joanna?'

'She's still at Latimer's, only now she's in charge of the division.'

'Good...so you're all fine?'

'I told you, we're all fine.'

'Good...'

'Christ, Ben, it's been four years. Didn't you get any of our letters?'

'I moved.'

'And you've never heard of redirection?'

'I moved in a hurry.'

'A moonlight flit?'

'Not quite. I like your outfit.'

He was wearing a white apron with undulating frills. He looked down at it, as if seeing it for the first time, and took it off, 'I was caramelising the crèmes brûlée.'

'I've missed dinner, then.'

'It's nine o'clock, of course you've missed dinner. Couldn't you have phoned?'

'Will, if it's awkward I'll just go.'

'You know I don't mean that?'

'Who is it, Will?' Joanna came into the hall. She stopped, looked at me as if I had come to con them into double-glazing. 'Ben?'

'The very same.'

'Will, you didn't say he was coming.'

'I didn't know, Jo. He's just turned up, out of the blue.'

'I like the house.'

She failed to take in what I had said. 'Out of the blue, after how long?'

'Four years,' said Will.

Then there was silence, a horrible silence where I wanted to go back to being the last man on earth. I was aware that I was hanging my head. Joanna was staring at me. Will looked awkward, as if he couldn't decide whose side he was on.

'Have you eaten?' he said.

'Not really.' In truth I was famished.

'I've made extra desserts. I must have known. Why don't you come on through.'

We went through to a low dining room with exposed beams and a brick fireplace. There were a table and chairs, showing the after-effects of a meal. I sat at the side. Joanna sat at the head. Will went into the kitchen.

She looked at me. There were things she wanted to say, but as of yet she wasn't ready. I felt like the last prawn on the plate.

Will came back with the desserts: little white ramekins set on white saucers.

'Sorry,' he said, 'I know these are supposed to have set cool, but they're still a little warm.'

I proffered the bottle of wine. 'The same goes for this. It's a Barsac, Doisy-Vedrines. It's really very good. Have you got any ice?'

Will took the bottle, 'Do we have any ice?' He looked at Joanna.

'We have ice,' she said.

I started on my dessert. It was impossibly rich and sweet. I felt like I should have asked for a sandwich first, but now would not be the time.

Will returned with an ice bucket. He uncorked the bottle and sniffed the open neck, then placed the bottle in the ice and let it sit. He went to a dresser and collected three little Paris goblets. He placed one in front of each of us and sat down to eat.

'How's little Will?' I said.

'Not so little,' said Will. 'He's up to Jo's shoulder.'

'Really? He was just a little ankle-biter.'

Joanna rolled the stem of the glass in her fingers. 'Well, Uncle Ben, even if you're not looking, children still grow up. He's already done his Grade Three piano.'

'I didn't know he played piano.'

She looked at me that way again. 'I know, Ben.'

Will poured the wine out. It was as good as the wine merchant had said it would be: sweet and complex and as smooth as an ice-cream soda.

'This is very good,' said Will, 'really, exceptionally good.'

I knew he would like it; I knew he would appreciate it.

'You must be doing all right to be able to afford something like this.'

'I'm doing okay.'

'So you are working?'

'Just at the moment, though I don't think it's going to last.'

'What is it?'

'Kind of import/export. It's a bit difficult to describe.'

'Keeps you out of the country, does it?' said Joanne.

An easy get-out, but I didn't deserve it easy, 'Not really.'

'Keeps you busy, though?'

'It's not too bad.'

We had all finished our desserts now. Will collected up the crockery and took it out to the kitchen.

Joanna slugged down the remainder of her glass, 'Ben, do you realise how worried he's been? You're his only brother. You're his only living relative. Couldn't you have phoned? Once a month? Once a year would have done. Just a post card, even.'

'I haven't really been myself.'

She was looking directly into my eyes, as if there was some sense to be made if she just looked deep enough. Will was standing in the doorway looking down. He looked the same way he did when I was fifteen and he was seventeen and Dad had caught me coming in at breakfast after a night out. I felt dirty. I could feel the presence of the road on my hands and face. I could feel the sweat in my armpits and grit in my eyes. I felt like a van driver pitched up and out of place amongst my own family. I remembered the whisky and felt more tired than ever, 'Would you mind if I had a bath? I've just realised what I must look like.'

I could see that they thought that this was a good idea. In a way I'd spoiled their meal. It had probably been special. Was it their anniversary? No, not in December.

'Use the bathroom at the end of the landing, you'll find a clean towel in the airing cupboard.'

I got up and walked towards the hall, 'Drink the rest of the wine, why don't you? I brought it for you.' Then I looked back, but not directly at either of them. 'Sorry,' I said.

The bath was cast-iron and had feet, like it could take me for a ride. I lay back and tried to soak myself out of my driving posture. I could feel myself frowning, so I found a flannel and draped it across my face, hoping to soak that out too. Everything went dark; I was lying in darkness, breathing through wet cotton. I could see the way Joanna had looked in her wedding dress, how she'd kept Will dancing despite his protestations. I listened for them downstairs, but it was too far for their voices to carry.

In the cool night air, still as a cat, the white van travelled quietly just above the surface of the road. Its wheels turned loosely in the drag. The note of the engine was a distant, subterranean hum, more vibration than sound. The van was the only white thing in a dark world. Where it had come from it could never return, where it was bound was beyond definition. It wasn't a good idea to go but, if it had to go, it would do so with all speed. Its white panels rippled like chiffon in the slipstream.

I must have slept for about half an hour. The water was still warm. My fingers were wrinkled. I got out, dried and put on a clean shirt. This was all too much: I probably shouldn't have come. I had to come. I couldn't not come.

Downstairs they had decamped to the living room. Will was sitting next to Joanna on the settee, in the same way he always did.

'Nice bath?'

'Thanks Will, I needed it.'

'So what's this job then? Is that your van or a works van?'

'Works van. I don't think you'd be very interested in the job.'

'Of course…'

'I don't think we need to know,' said Joanna.

Awkward. We sat like that for a long time, until it was

time for the news. Will always watched the news at 10:30. So we sat in front of the television and it was as if I had been away for two days. Not that I could take it in. I saw the news, but registered none of it.

Joanna brought in a pot of tea and poured me a cup to my usual specifications without even having to ask. How was it possible to feel this uncomfortable in so much comfort?

At eleven-fifteen Joanna went to bed. I knew Will wouldn't be far behind.

'I've made up one of the spare beds, the room next to the bathroom. I imagine you'll be wanting to stay the night.'

'Thanks. I should have said. If it's any trouble. I'll be gone early in the morning.'

'Of course it's not any trouble, you're family.'

Five minutes afterwards Will got up, as I knew he would. I kept my eyes on the television.

'Look, Ben,' he said, 'Jo and I have been talking. We wanted you to know you'd be welcome to come for Christmas. We're not up to much. Jo's parents are coming. We'd like you to come.'

Whatever shrivelled kernel of heart I had left burst at that precise moment, 'Thanks Will, I'll see.'

LAST DAY

I lay awake in the early hours trying to digest the huge sandwich I'd made after my hosts had gone to bed, trying to digest the thoughts driving headlong through my mind.

Things have a strange way of being triggered. I'd been taken aback by finding the photograph of Gail amongst my things. I hadn't seen her for years though, of course, I was aware of her presence. But I'd managed not to let it bother me. All that stuff belonged to Ben and he'd been left far behind. I was an autonomous force who needed no one. I'd been delivering boxes for the best part of three years. I delivered packages on my bike when Terence asked me to. That was all I was about. Nevertheless, for no reason I could divine, the image of Gail as she was then wouldn't leave me alone. I started to wonder where she'd got to. I began to picture her as she might be now. Then I saw her on the street.

I'd taken a package up east and I was returning via Shepherd's Bush during the busiest part of the day. I was feeling a bit listless, so I wasn't even bothering to thread my way through the traffic. The August heat was baking me in my leathers and the still air stank of fumes and hot oil.

Gail walked past me on the pavement, carrying a file. I saw her coming, because she was walking in the opposite way to the way I was travelling. She was carrying a file, but I didn't see that straight away. She was wearing a skirt. 'Nice legs,' I thought. She was wearing a green jacket that matched her skirt. I saw her face and thought that everything matched and, by then, she had passed by and I had turned my attention back to the job in hand. It was a couple of minutes before I thought again.

You can look at someone for the first time and they can seem instantly familiar. Somehow they fit into an idea that you have already formed in your head. I don't know what it all means, except that I'm sure that the very first time I saw Gail there was no period of adjustment, only an instant of recognition. When I saw her again it was like looking at someone I'd always known and, for that reason, it took me two minutes to register who it actually was. When I realised, everything came to a stop, from paying attention to the traffic to drawing my next breath.

I pulled the bike onto the pavement and shut it down. A passer by looked at me in disgust. I didn't care. I looked around and then started to walk back the way I'd come.

How far can someone walk in two minutes? How long is two minutes when you're not counting? In any case, she was gone. I walked faster. I was hot in my helmet. I took it off.

I had no idea what I was going to say. I don't even think that I planned to say anything. It was just that I couldn't have her walk straight past me and leave it at that.

I kept on down the pavement. The junction of the Uxbridge Road: choice. I looked in all directions. I looked for the green jacket: nothing. I looked at the ground, my head full of thoughts, thinking nought. Without resolving anything I started walking west, past Shepherd's Bush tube. For some reason I knew she wasn't on the Underground. I stepped up my pace a little, faster than the people around me. Ideas fell from my head until the only thing left was this desire to see again a green jacket in the midst of all this limitless expanse of humanity. Too hot for walking in leathers.

If I'd have had time to think about it I might have stayed on the bike. I could have let Gail remain a disembodied voice in the ether and carried on in the universe into which I'd fallen, but I didn't have time. I was knocked off my bike by the suddenness of her appearance. I may have had the apparatus to deal with occurrences like that once in my life, but that life had been flushed out of my system.

I kept on for half a mile. I remembered how fast she walked. I would have to catch her up. I don't know why, but I knew that she had come this way. I kept the pace up. Sweat was running down my collar. Everything had been subsumed into this single image of the green jacket. I kept on going until a new idea forced itself through. I stopped. What if she had stepped into one of the dozens of buildings that I'd already walked past? I looked backwards for an answer and then along to route ahead, to what now looked like a hopeless task. My breath was heavy and I could feel the sweat in my scalp. I stood on the pavement, getting in the way as people I had pushed past pushed past me and, at that very moment, she emerged from the doorway of the bakery right next to where I was standing. She had her file in one hand and a paper bag in the other. For a fraction of a second she saw me, looked directly into my face without a spark of recognition. She continued on her way. How could she not recognise me? Then the door of the bakery closed and I caught sight of my reflection in its glass. I saw only John.

I sat on a low wall a little way down the street from where she lived. I knew she lived there because she'd opened the door with a key. We were only a couple of streets away from the tumult of the Uxbridge Road, but here it was largely quiet, as if nothing happened anywhere. The low wall was shaded by a tree, which partially hid me from view. The sweating had left me thirsty. In another universe I could go up and knock on the door and ask kindly for a drink of water. Five fifteen – I was waiting to see if anyone else was going to be coming home from work.

At some point the light went and the sweat on my neck

felt cold. In however many hours it was I hadn't thought of anything. It wasn't just the darkness that had overtaken me. I was hungry and thirsty and I needed a piss. Only the last thing, though, was going to get me to move. All my energy was going on erecting barriers in my brain. Something had to be kept out. What? I couldn't tell, because the blockade was being successful. That was enough. Time to move. I walked carefully along the street, feeling like I didn't belong. I really didn't belong. Gail's light was on in the downstairs room. The blinds were open and I could see inside. I slowed right down and looked in. She wasn't there, just a normal home with normal things: a maroon settee, book shelves in the alcoves by the fireplace, an archway through to the dining room, another window onto whatever lay unseen at the back of the house. I felt as if I could see right through her life, but that was it. I was looking through without my eyes settling on any truth other than that no one else had come home. I had been as close to this person as I had to anyone in my life. Even with the years elapsed between then and now I couldn't believe I knew so little. I didn't even know that she lived in London, though I suppose I could have guessed. I hadn't suspected for a million years that I would ever see her again. She had become a disembodied voice. Now I knew where she lived, what clothes she wore to a meeting.

I stopped in a burger joint to use the facilities on my way back to the bike. I felt like a shadow under the glare of their fluorescent lights, as if the light were strong enough to pass straight through a spectral figure like myself. I didn't go to places where the lights were bright.

For a hot night the air felt chilly, but it was still air, like the air when time stops. Amazingly, the bike was where I'd left it – no ticket, nothing missing. I got on and rode off nowhere. I wasn't ready to go home yet.

I packed my bag quietly in Will's spare bedroom and went downstairs. I washed my face in the kitchen sink and made do with a mug of milk for breakfast. It was just six o'clock.

I'd nearly made it to the door before I noticed Will sitting on the stairs. Shouldn't have run the tap.

'You're up early,' he said.

'So are you.'

'Earlier than I'd like.'

'You didn't have to see me off.'

'No.'

'Goodbye then.'

He took a moment. It was too early for both of us. 'See you, Ben.'

'Yeah.'

MIST

I put on distance as quickly as I could. The last vestiges of Ben drained from my attitude and John took back control of the wheel. Tarporley, tarpaulin: a big square of green canvas draped over the crashed remains of a motorcycle. If there had been an ambulance it had been and gone. Two policemen stood in the mist waiting for something. Blood – the sheet protects us from visions of our own mortality. Just show us – it's the truth for all of us. Did the rider overcook it on the last bend or was he knocked off, in classic style, by some twat emerging from the upcoming junction who 'just didn't see him'? I passed by in slow motion, trying to look while trying not to look, equating what I could see with my own experience of spills and thrills, getting too close to the tanker as a consequence and having to back off. Days go on in the same vein in which they start. How fucking telling.

After the move to the new unit something changed with Terence and Dave. You could tell it was what they'd been after for a long time. They swanked about the place like they'd just won control of BP. It was just a standard business barn with a suite of offices, but it was their barn. They ordered in new carpets and black-ash veneer furniture, computers and phones and went about making the place as comfortable as possible. Not much came with us: a dozen files and the last few aerospace spades. The life of the workshop was gone, and the dirt that went with it.

After the furniture came the entertainment: a midi hi-fi and the biggest television I had ever seen. When T and D weren't conducting business they were watching TV. More often than not they were watching videos and DVDs. They watched Westerns and pornography, the inevitable Arnie features, but mostly, I noticed, every type of gangster flick. There was that thirties and forties stuff with Cagney and George Raft, American and French film noir, *Il Borsolino*, *Point Blank* and *The Killers*, *The Outfit* with Robert Duval and Joe Don Baker, *Scarface*, *The Untouchables*, *Miller's Crossing*, *Casino* and a host of others. But by far the most popular was *Goodfellas*. I could bet, if I was called in, that when I got there and they weren't busy with something else they would be busy watching *Goodfellas* for the thousandth time, sat rapt in front of it, smiling knowingly at each other at key points in the narrative, chortling under their breath like two pubescent boys at the point in a sex education film where an actress demonstrates her breasts for purposes of enlightenment.

I didn't much care what they were doing for entertainment. I got money. I got time to myself. Eventually I got Dawn and that sorted that. The route started out as an easy, two-day thing, but soon stretched to three. I liked it. For the first time in my working life no one was behaving like a boss. They gave me a mobile phone so that they could keep tabs, but in all this time it's never rung. These days I keep it in my bag, charged and ready to go, but always mute. They know I'll get the job done. I know I'll get the job done. The job always gets done. Sitting in a jam on the A49 doesn't seem to be getting it done, but the driver always finds a way.

It was a couple of days after I'd discovered where Gail lived that I found myself amongst the firs at the bottom of her garden. It was not yet totally dark, but dark enough that I'd been able to hide myself in the shadows as I'd traversed the neighbouring gardens to get there. The gardens backed on to those of the row behind, leaving me near to the centre of a large oasis of green. At the boundary of the two sets of gardens ran a wall. It wasn't intact in all places and had been supplemented with shrubs and trees and bits of fencing to maintain the integrity of the plots. So there were risks involved, but it had still been possible to arrive at my vantage point without being seen.

The bottom of Gail's garden featured a row of leylandii, maybe twenty-five feet high, mirrored in the garden behind by a similar row. A dispute, I thought, sometime in the past, in which both sets of occupants tried to shut each other out. The two rows had grown into each other to form a thick mass. Through the middle of the mass ran the wall and, on the wall, me.

It had taken quite some time to find a good position. Only in one or two places could I see through the foliage towards the house and only one of these had a decent view. At one point I could stand and see into the kitchen, at another I could sit and look directly into the dining room window and through to the lounge. It wasn't a great view – I couldn't see the entire room – but a big enough slice of it to see if anyone was passing through or if the TV had been switched on.

I had been looking out for anyone new, but it was clear that Gail lived alone. The way the suite was arranged gave that away. The chairs faced each other, ready to receive visitors in conversation, not a family focussed on the box. The general way the interior of the house looked to me seemed like the work of only one hand. I hadn't seen anyone else. I had hardly seen Gail. Twice she had walked through my field of vision to the kitchen, turned on the light, done something for four or five minutes and walked back. There was a light on in one of the windows upstairs. I had found a vantage point to get a view of this window, but the curtain was drawn. Not a bedroom: I already knew where the bedroom was. Not a bathroom, because that was behind the narrow pane of textured glass over to the right. It had to be her study, or office.

I looked at the time, but it was too dark to see the hands of my watch in the thick of the tree fronds. I tried to work out what the time might be, considering the time of year and the level of light. Then I couldn't remember the date, only that it was sometime in the second half of October. I was a fool to have lost track.

Whatever Gail did in her office took a long time and needed enough concentration to require two coffees. Gail took four or five minutes to make a coffee. She had a kitchen routine: filling the kettle first – just enough for one mug, coffee, milk, then mix them together with a spoon, lean against the counter watching the kettle boil with a blank look that nevertheless said that there were thoughts going on inside, watching the steam rise from the kettle, hearing it click off and then remaining still for a few seconds until the bubbling water calmed down. Always this moment waiting, as if to remind herself that she was not at the beck and call of a kitchen appliance. How many times had I seen this? It had been too much of a struggle to get to the kitchen viewpoint and see tonight, but I knew the routine. I could picture it in my head and translate it to this new location.

It wasn't mist, it was fog and it wasn't clearing, even with the daylight. Coming down the 49 was a bad idea. I checked the dash clock for the third time in as many minutes and tutted to myself. Whitchurch had been a pain, but at least I had left Cheshire.

Preston Brockhurst, Hadnall – very little to see. There was a blacksmith's – you don't see many of those, but the scenery was occluded by ground-cloud. Progress was awkward: every time I got free it was reduced visibility again or I got stuck behind another tosser doing thirty-five, burning out my retinae with his fog-lights. There were precious few places to pass. Then there were these ivy-covered trees looming at the side of the road like frozen giants.

I have been down here in summer, long before I worked for T & D. What a difference the seasons make. This trip is the ultimate trip, why can't it just go right?

Now I have to think about Will and Joanna. It was so easy when I could pretend they weren't there, when I knew they had gone from the old place and I had no frame of reference to picture the new.

Will looked well. So did Joanna. They seem to have grasped something that's escaping John at this moment. It's one of those things where you're aware of a presence, but can't figure out its shape. John is a know-it-all kind of guy, so why is he falling short here.

Shrewsbury, tiring of all the urban traffic. Who wants towns and cities? You want free space and open views. Only the clear road leads to the clear head. After Shrewsbury it's Church Stretton and Wenlock edge. I should be on holiday here, not clock-watching and dicing.

I stopped for diesel at the only garage in the country that didn't sell stuff to eat. The world felt damp from the fog. I was trying to be quick, but the two wagons I had passed back down the road re-passed me just as I was pulling away from the pump. Wagons have to keep on the roll – the difference in consumption between steady progress and braking and accelerating can mean the difference between profit and loss on a job. That's why I always let wagons out on the motorway: so they don't lose momentum. For my job the margins are so high I could throw fuel away.

I caught up with the wagons again and angled for a way to pass.

Often, when I went down to the unit, Specca would be there. I still wasn't sure for whom he worked, or exactly why he had to be around so much, but whatever it was involved a fair amount of covert chin-wagging with Terence and Dave. I knew that he was something to do with the route of supply. If we were distributors then he worked for either the importer or the original manufacturer. He was scruffy to look at, and none too bright, but he gave the impression that there was something more significant backing him up. No one seemed to think I needed enlightening and, despite my innate curiosity, I was kind of glad. My experience has not always been that knowledge is power, but I've been around long enough to know that the wrong type of knowledge can give others power over you. I'm happy to get on with my bit of responsibility and leave it at that.

So, Specca didn't concern me too much, even if he did make a show of fronting it out if he crossed my path, like we were back in the playground.

'He's a cunt, that Specca,' said Dave one day, apropos of nothing.

'Is he?' I said.

'Oh yeah, he's a right cunt.'

I didn't enquire any further – Dave was always ready with an opinion – though later I had cause to think again.

I'm beginning to wonder whether John might not be a bit of a fool. I suppose it could be down to his youth – he's barely three, after all. I can't quite see how he's got himself into this position. Each step of the way is clear; the whole route is not. It's clear that it's a journey of sorts; it's not clear what has provided the motive power.

I overtook the wagons again, taking a big risk. Naturally, the moment I had passed we reached the Ludlow Bypass and they turned off into the town. It made no difference, five minutes later I was stuck behind another queue. One thing is true: you can never make better time than the person ahead of you.

It's kind of a shame this is the last trip. I feel like I've really settled into the job. I know what has to be done; I know the extent of my responsibilities. I'm just an employee, paid to do a job. At the top of the tree there are people who deal with policy. All this is down to choices they have made, using their judgement of proper practice.

On the road you are your own boss when you're behind the wheel. Or at least you can kid yourself that that's the case. It's a kind of negotiation you make with yourself: pretending on one hand that you have freedom of choice while all the choices are merely details of someone else's design. For the moment, then, I forget Terence and Dave and try to put myself somewhere else. Yet I've had nothing to eat and the pit that's opened up at the base of my stomach is filling up with acid. I've barely averaged thirty miles an hour since I started and I should be in Ludlow now, looking for something to fill my face. Instead, I've got to make up time.

OVERLAP

I found out how to follow someone.

You have to think of it in zones. We all occupy zones. The most fundamental one is our own personal space, the small balloon of universe immediately surrounding us. Unless you're really preoccupied, or in a very crowded place like right in the front at a major gig, you're usually pretty aware of what's going on in this space. In the normal course of events you can detect changes in the flux within it, such as an individual entering for interaction. This is Zone One: a zone occupied by one, for the purposes of one only, the sole exception being for the occasion of sexual congress, when two Zone Ones combine to form a single, dual zone with a single, shared boundary, within it a set of common elements, a collision of cultures with all it's potential joys and inherent hazards. If you're the follower, then you may never impinge upon this zone. The follower cannot be seen, must not be detected.

The next one out is Zone Two: your immediate, observable environment. This is fluid. It can vary in size from the box room you've gone into to look for a file, to the field you are ploughing. For most people on a city street it's the few yards out in any direction, wherein there are things with which you may have to interact. Certainly, you have to be more or less aware of what is going on in this environment, because it's the place where most phenomena that are going to have an immediate effect on you are likely to occur.

Zone Two overlaps with Zone Three: the general environment in which you are situated or through which you are moving. Mostly, there are not immediate consequences for you at the outer limits of this zone but, closer to or, as things become closer, those consequences tend to take on the significance of Zone Two phenomena. A city zone is very much different to a woodland zone or a parliamentary zone during a civil insurrection. There are secure zones, like the inside of your house when you've locked yourself in for the night, and unsecured ones, like the tube system you've fought through to get there. When you're in need of it, Zone Two will expand into Zone Three, like when you're surveying the next section of your mountain ascent or when you're looking out for the appropriate entrance for the building in which you have an appointment. The stretching of Zone Two will generally follow your line of sight, unless you are under threat from a sniper or something and attempting to perceive the environment with holographic perception.

Zone Four is the unperceived environment outside One, Two and Three, like the town you're in, or the motorway you're on, or the county or the country. Zone Five is Outer Space or something like that.

The task of the follower, then, is to keep the followed within your own Zone Two without getting inside the Zone Two of the followed, their sphere of awareness. If, for any reason, this should occur, then they have to make sure they can proceed unnoticed, or have a gambit for getting safely back to Zone Three as quickly as possible. Zone One is obviously right out.

The follower is on a piece of invisible elastic, linked directly to the followed, sometimes stretched out, sometimes drawn in. The followed can't know about the link or the game is stopped. To the follower the link is the primary consideration. This can be the worst element, because it makes the followed into the one who drives events. The follower becomes a passenger in the back of the vehicle of another's existence; his movements are prefigured by the decision making and practices of someone else.

Even with this, I liked seeing Gail. I liked to see again how she moved, what shop windows caught her eye on a casual walk down the street. I liked to see her waiting for a bus, even though that meant I was going to lose sight of her for a spell. I liked to see her changes of clothes, whether she was putting her hair up in a business-like way that day or whether she was going to let it flow with a mind of its own like she used to do back when.

I thought of each outing as a mission, in which the goal was for me to connect with her zone structure, stay connected with it for whatever time and see where she took me. I looked for points of resonance in her life. I tried to register what sort of things she liked to eat; how much time she liked to spend at home; how much out; when she was putting in extra time at work; when she was just passing time. Each time I wondered whether she was even slightly aware that there was someone out there watching her back if she were to get into danger. She was often so thoughtful that I could get quite close, always outside what she was thinking, often close enough to see the curve of her wrist. One day I spent an hour with her in a park near her house while she ate a sandwich in the September sunshine. Who was she thinking of, in that hour, eating olives with a cocktail stick on her day off? At night, if conditions were right, I could find my way along to her garden wall and watch her, watching TV and making her way occasionally to the kitchen or to the bathroom or to the unknown room upstairs.

She was thinking of *him*. On a Friday night, in the rain, I saw him.

In the trees I was safe from the worst of the downpour. Still, Gail's house looked warm inside, orange light coming through from the living room, through the dining room, emanating into the garden.

I'd kept away from her evenings out. She would have lots of friends. I didn't want to see friends together. I liked most that it was about her and me. When she was at home it was more like that and, of course, it's easier to keep tabs on someone who remains in the same place. It gives you the option for independent movement:

walking slowly past the front window for an alternative view; riding past on the bike when she's leaving the house.

I was now quite good at getting into the garden. I'd found a better way to see into the kitchen that required less relocation. I liked her home. It looked lived in, well thought out, an extension of her personality.

She was alone until half nine. I'd been watching her for two hours. The bike was parked a couple of streets away as usual. She came in from work and spent some time in the bathroom. When she came down she had changed into something nice, but not the sort of outfit she would wear for going out. She ate a salad, slowly, while she sat at the dining table reading through something that looked like a report, every now and again turning back through the pages to reread a section, looking up into the corner of the room for a thought, returning to the text.

It was nice when she ate at the table, even though she made the big table look empty. She was close to the window, closer to me. When she looked out through the window I was there, right at the limit of her second zone. With a small motion of a hand I could enter into it, without I was irrevocably outside, comfortable in the safety of Zone Three.

He arrived at exactly nine-thirty, after she'd taken the empty plate out to the kitchen and dabbed the corners of her mouth with a tissue. The way she did it made me wonder whether she was wearing lipstick.

The rain was coming in hard when she brought him through to the living room, a dark-haired man dressed for business. He had brought a bottle of wine – a claret shaped bottle, probably Australian. She seemed pleased. She went to the kitchen for glasses. He made himself comfortable on the settee. She came back. She opened the bottle and filled the glasses. I thought I saw her smile. They were talking about something. It made him smile. She had the report thing in her hand. She went to sit in one of the armchairs. They talked some more. The rain was making it more difficult to see through the glass. I leant forward a little. She came to the window. I leant back. For the first time I'd seen, she closed the curtains. I waited for one moment in the now dark garden. I took up and left, wet.

I kept myself at home for a couple of days, passing time with television until I couldn't watch another thing or face another bottle of wine. I felt my system clogging up with fat and digestive residues. I began to imagine my bloodstream overcome with particulate matter. My sweat felt oily. I tried to drink water. My body cried out for activity.

Outside on the street the humidity was keeping the fumes close to the ground. The air stank of traffic and industry. No better weather was forthcoming. I walked for a long time without success. Everything was about keeping Gail out of my head. Nothing was working.

I started to think in three dimensions. What if zones

could be layered, so that you could set your layer beneath that of someone else? Or above it? What if you could interleave your zones between others, into a private space of your own, so that there could never be an overlap? Then no one would ever be able to touch you. No one would ever be able to get close enough to have an effect. Then you'd be home free.

'Won't be needing you for a couple of days,' said Dave.

'Right,' I said.

'But we're going to have a job for you soon enough.'

'Back on the route?'

'Another job. You're up for that?'

'Whatever.'

Then he unfolded a big bunch of bills from his back pocket and gave me about a third of them. I didn't count how much – the best part of a grand, probably. It was just money. But then I started thinking, as I was climbing on to the bike, why don't you just get away for a couple of days? Find somewhere new on the map and take a holiday? Go somewhere where it doesn't matter if your zones overlap – nice hotel, looking out of the window at the sea, decent food on the doorstep, taking in the scenery without being on a schedule, travelling on your own time. By the time I was half way home I'd pretty well convinced myself. I was on to a good thing. Then I pulled up next to a car at the lights with its window open and the radio up way too loud and within the hour I was back out, heading towards Gail's.

EPPING

'What's up with you?' Dawn said, as we lay on the floor of her living room with our clothes strewn around us.

'What do you mean, what's up?'

'You're miles away.'

'Am I?' I might have been, 'Nothing's up.'

I propped myself up against the settee and tried to shake myself back to the moment. I didn't know it then, at the end of October, that I had only two trips to go. This trip had been a pain right from the outset. I was tired starting out. I'd stayed out way too late at Gail's; I was dog tired by the time I got to Dawn's.

She looked at me closely. She seemed a little dark under the eyes. I wondered whether the other John had been giving her a hard time. Suddenly I wanted to wipe him from the face of the earth. I could have done it and got away with it. I didn't want her noticing my state of mind. She could change the subject. I felt like closing my eyes for a long time and falling off somewhere else. Dawn wasn't having it. She pulled herself up close and put a hand on my stomach. My muscles tensed.

'Come on, John.' She kissed me and our sweat mingled again.

'Sorry,' I said, 'just tired.'

She moved her hand.

'Thirsty.' I went to stand up.

She stopped me, 'I'll get you a beer.'

'No thanks, just water.'

She went to the kitchen. I tried not to hate myself for wanting her out of the way for a minute. I didn't like the fact that she could read me, not even a little. John liked to be unreachable. I started to put my clothes back on, even though we would be going up to bed anytime.

The extra job that Dave had talked about required me to be down at the unit one lunchtime with a suit to change into. Dave and Terence were already in their suits when I got there.

'You'll be driving,' said Terence, handing me the keys to his Merc.

'You sure?' I said. Stupid question: Terence didn't do unsure.

They both got in the back. I could tell there was something up. Dave wasn't saying too much and he only usually kept his mouth shut when his brain was dealing with something significant.

I don't really get on with automatics – you're robbed of some of your elements of control. I can see the advantages in stop-start city traffic, yet I can't get away from the feeling that part of the decision making process has already been done by boffins in a lab somewhere reaching a rough consensus on change intervals. Gear change by committee – I don't like being second-guessed by anyone. Also, I end up with a left foot itching for something to do that can only be kept still by conscious effort.

It was a long trip. We could have gone round the M25, but Terence's directions took us the urban route, round the North Circular. We even pissed around on the A104 rather than taking the M11. Except for the occasional instruction from Terence it was quiet inside the car. We kept the entertainment turned off, which suited me fine. I could see them in the rear view mirror, stock still in their grey flannel, keeping cool in the climate-controlled atmosphere. I wondered whether I should be wearing a cap.

I could feel us nearing our destination – the air was heating up. I got the feeling that we were getting outside our territory, even though I'd not been aware that we had one. We were the Westerners, heading up East. We had to be on our guard. I was there either to swell the numbers or for the sake of appearances, that they were too important to be doing their own driving.

We crossed the boundary of the M25 and headed off towards Harlow, past Epping Forest. I could see Dave working his mouth with his tongue. A couple more directions from Terence – off the main road, onto a minor one, onto a farm track; at the end of the track a set of dilapidated, red-brick agricultural buildings. On instruction, I pulled up the car on some wasted ground about forty yards short. We got out.

'You'll stay here,' said Terence.

They started off towards the door of the nearest brick shed. It opened. I could hear the sound of a generator. Someone came out to meet them. They went in. The door closed behind them and the sound of the generator was gone. I stood alone at the edge of a field in my best business suit with a light breeze ruffling the autumn sunshine.

Time moved on. Business. I felt like I'd got all dressed up for a cancelled wedding. I didn't like the time it was taking. I didn't much like that I didn't know what it was about. I felt exposed in the open air.

Something about having been moving makes it difficult to keep still. Without thinking I'd started to amble off. I steered away from the building that had received Terence and Dave. Wind currents made patterns in the uncut meadow next to the track, speaking of meanings in an unknown language. I walked around the generator building to the sheds behind. It was all looking run-down, like farm buildings often do, though it looked to me like no actual farm work had gone on here for a long time. Most of the land had probably been swallowed up by development. All that were left here were the last vestiges of another type of land use.

I went inside a long building and mooched around. There were the concrete troughs where cattle had fed, but nothing else other than empty feed sacks and a mat of straw and dust decades old. I had a look inside the other buildings: a similar story. I crept out towards the boundary of the plot, around the back of the last building, to find a vehicle graveyard.

There was an old Fergie tractor that should probably be in the hands of a collector; a rusted-to-buggery Comma van. Behind that a row of three cars nesting in the long grass: a Mark II Escort; a flat-four Citrôen of some description; a tired old Cavalier just like the one I used to drive. The front window was out. I looked past the moss-green window rubbers into the weathered interior. I saw Ben in the driver's seat, not far into his twenties. He stared back. The car stared back at me, the bottomless, vacant stare of a skull at an archaeological exhibition. I expected, at any moment, that the engine would start up and tell me something, but there was nothing.

Suddenly I didn't like what I was feeling. Time had gone without me noticing and I hadn't been paying attention to the job. I started back towards the car, past the empty buildings, round a corner, straight into Specca.

I tried to continue, but there was some long streak of piss behind him, who I hadn't seen before, manoeuvring himself to get in my way. Specca was in my way.

'What the fuck are you doing?'

I just looked at him.

'I said, what the fuck are you doing?'

'What's it look like I'm doing?'

Not very bright, Specca, probably didn't answer many questions at school, probably didn't get on with questions unless he was asking them. In any case, I didn't have to answer to him. I bypassed him and his mate and continued on my way back to the car. They followed me, like ducks. I tried to take my time: no one likes to be hurried. Dave and Terence were standing by the car when I got back.

'Where the fuck were you?' said Dave.

'I had to take a piss.'

Terence said nothing. Specca and his other half kept their distance. Dave was looking slightly agitated.

'Okay,' he said, 'let's get the fuck out of here.'

Dawn came back with the water. I'd managed to get as far as putting on my trousers. My belt was still hanging loose.

'Thanks,' I said

I took the glass and drank it back. The water felt ice cold after the heat we'd been generating, too much of a contrast. She was still naked. I wondered whether anyone had been able to see her through the kitchen window: it didn't have a blind. Standing naked looks odd when it doesn't have a purpose. It shouldn't do – we're all supposed to be natural creatures – but it does. I wanted her to put something on, a dressing gown, anything. She waited until I'd finished the drink. I looked down on her for a moment, with the empty glass in my hand.

'More?' she said.

'No more,' I said, 'thanks.'

I laid the glass on the coffee table. She came over and

pressed herself against me, both of us standing in the middle of the living room carpet. She pulled me close and I felt the flutter of her eyelashes on my chest.

'I can't hear your heartbeat,' she said.

'You're listening in the wrong place.'

'You're a fucker, John, you know that?'

'How else would you have me?'

'You know what I mean, always coming and going, you don't like the place you live, your job's keeping you on the road all the time.'

'Everyone has to make a living.'

'You could make a living anywhere. You could make a living here.'

'In sunny Stockton? What would I do?'

'I don't know. People always need stuff delivered, don't they? There's got to be jobs for professional drivers. If you don't want to drive anymore, there must be lot of jobs around for someone like you. You could do a job with regular hours and find a place to live.'

'What sort of place?'

She kissed my chest, 'You know what sort.'

Hell is in the unsaid; the devil is in the detail. If conditions were right you could go a lifetime without talking to anyone else. In that lifetime nothing on your external world would ever get resolved, yet everything inside would be clear cut and easily manageable. It's when people send you messages that it all gets difficult, because than it's all compromise, a low-level negotiation between two sets of requirements. There's a lifetime of joy and pain to be had in trying to reconcile all the issues, without ever having a full set of evidence to hand. It's all there between the lines, but how do you read a blank space in someone else's script? How could she know that I was too far gone for that? My script was strictly controlled. I was careful to fill in the gaps so there was no space to do any reading between.

Her hands were patterns on my back, gripping my flesh in an attempt to make us one. My primary zone had shrunk to its smallest ever dimensions: it reached no further than the surface of my skin.

'What about John?' I said, 'What would you do about him?'

'I don't know.'

'You know you'd have to do something.'

'I know, I don't...'

'So?'

The nature of her grip had changed. Even I couldn't be as bad as that.

'Tell you what,' I said, 'I could use that beer now.'

'Yeah, I'll get it.'

We disengaged and she went back out to the kitchen. I tightened my belt and sat back down on the settee. She came back with an opened bottle of beer, like a naked hand-servant. The act broke the tension of the mood, at least for her. I took the beer and swallowed back.

'I'm going up,' she said, 'you coming?'

'I'll be up soon.'

'Don't be long. I've got plans for you.'

'No, I've just got to check the roadwork reports on teletext.'

She knelt on the settee and leant towards me, folded me in her arms while I held the bottle at arms length for safety, 'Come on, don't be long.'

She squeezed my leg, got up and headed for the stairs. I took a swig of beer and searched around for the remote.

I watched some shit on the TV for half an hour, slowly drawing on the contents of the bottle. When it was empty I took it into the kitchen and stared out of the window, into the unseeing darkness. I went back into the living room and slowly gathered up the remainder of my clothes, climbed quietly up stairs and through to the bedroom where, luckily, she was asleep.

LEOMINSTER

A49 Ludlow bypass, Ashford Bowdler, Brimfield. The fog sagged across the road in thick drifts. For a moment it would be partially clear and then impenetrable once again. Sometimes fog is a creature with malevolent intent. Still, its presence lends a mystery to familiar places, creating hidden corners out of open spaces.

We were crawling along. I had my wipers on intermittent, because the fog was gripping the windscreen. Hard going. The fog lights of the twat in front were boring holes in my eyes. Fog lights are designed as a warning to the approaching driver, once you've approached it's like looking into Vulcan's fiery furnace. Times two. You can flash and beep all you want, no one ever gets the message.

Crawling along in fog has very little to do with driving – it's like being a carriage in a train. The engine in front is making all the decisions. At the same time you have to concentrate hard. The mind wants to be in control, so it occupies itself with the minutiae of everything that's available to the eye: the texture of the road; the status of the white lines; the comings and goings of bends and junctions. A bad driver will just fix his attention on the taillights of the guy in front and forget about all the rest. People like that tend to get too close. They have surrendered control and are looking for an accident.

Now I was really hungry. It had been hours since I'd left Will's. I was in unfamiliar territory and I was almost certainly running late, though I couldn't quite tell, because I'd never tried it this way. I must surely be nearing Leominster, but with the fog there's no time to stop. Making progress through fog is a war of attrition, where progress is measured in feet rather than miles.

Time to turn on the radio. Gigi will be coming on for the afternoon shift anytime and, as if by magic...

"...tailbacks on the M6, drivers should use dipped headlights and, on the A38 Aston Expressway, there are major delays owing to an accident on the ring road there, with traffic trailing back off the slip road. In Nottinghamshire there are major hold-ups on the A60 northbound, heading towards Mansfield, because of road works and further north, in Scotland, Long Tom has called in from the M8 at Livingston. He'd like to apologise to all those drivers stuck behind his oversized load, which is currently heading west. He says he's going as fast as he can, but there's only so fast you can manage with more than a hundred tons of grain silo sitting on the back. That's it, I'll be back in half an hour with the next report."

"Thank you, Gail, we'll look forward to seeing you then."

It was rather a surprise to learn that there are media

types. I had always assumed that success in the media was a destination available equally to all. You worked your way up in your chosen field and, if you got lucky, you got promoted to the inner sanctum of fame and remuneration. Thus, you banged away on electric guitar for two years in your dad's garage, with four like-minded mates, gigged around locally and then nationally, until you finally got noticed by some A & R mandarin and landed yourself a record contract. If you then managed to get around enough, were able to grab people's attention with your home-grown talent you might even get yourself a measure of success. Likewise for other fields of artistic endeavour. Most often, though, nothing like this is the case. Half the tossers you see on Top of the Pops have already been through a lifetime of stage school, teenage modelling, being fourth munchkin in pantomime in Southend-on-Sea, walk-on parts on Grange Hill, singing badly in the chorus of a West End musical before blagging a gig as part of a soon-to-be all-conquering girl band, supposedly direct from the street, overflowing with style and attitude. And your first quote? 'I've been into music since I was four years old. I was always singing in the house and I wrote my first song when I was seven. I always knew I was going to make it.' Kismet, darling – which four-year-old isn't singing around the house? Who hasn't made up something to sing, even if it's only substitute lyrics for a popular tune? As for destiny, we all occupy ourselves with daydreams of our forthcoming success. Our society makes a currency out of celebrity and a damnation out of the opposite. There is no greater insult than to be thought of as a nobody, so we all try to see ourselves, some of the time, silhouetted in the xenon flare of fame because, historically that's where all the cash and tropical holidays and unrestricted fantasy sex is going on. So, destiny is a mother who works as a producer for the BBC and a leg-up as a media baby.

Of course, she wasn't called Gail Gee when I knew her. Gee must be her stage name for Equity or something. Makes a good pun – Gail Gee, G.Gee., Gigi – memorable for radio.

I heard her for the first time at the end of the summer. I was in the van, on the route. It was easy going that time, at least up the M1. Everyone must have been on holiday.

I didn't take much notice at first: she was using a radio voice. I hadn't heard her voice for years, but somewhere in my head a register of her rhythms and cadences must have remained. Even though the traffic report was a kind of performance, the underlying structure of the way she was speaking must have been the same.

I was just passing Leeds, heading for the A1, so I had the radio turned up to see if there was any trouble brewing further up – sometimes, when you've had a clear run on the swings, you get held up on the roundabouts. It was only after she'd finished the report that it sank in. I'd been thinking, in an abstract way, what a nice voice that was for telling you about trouble, when I suddenly realised that it was a nice voice because it was Gail's.

I pulled off at the next junction and found somewhere to park up. Memory should be invited, it shouldn't come up and hit you in the back of the neck while you're driving. Suddenly I didn't feel like I could marshal all my powers of concentration. I got out of the van and shook my head. You don't really expect your ex-girlfriends to be talking to you through the radio. That sort of thing can upset your sense of reality. Had I daydreamed it? No way. She had spoken to me over the airwaves and now I was forming mental pictures. You always try to put a face to a voice. Sometimes the face you put to someone you've heard on the radio, or only ever spoken to on the phone, doesn't tally with what they actually look like. Even if you find out, at a later date, what they're actually like, something of that first, imagined face remains. But I knew what Gail looked like or, at least, how she used to look. Now I had to try and visualise something that had no part in my existence. I spent the rest of the trip trying to put things together, then made myself tired trying not to. I could listen to a different station. By the time I got back I had it all sorted out then, two days later, her picture dropped out of the book I was holding and I was hooked. I listened out for her on the radio even when I wasn't out on the road and, sometimes when I did, when she had finished her report and was engaged in some witty badinage with the presenter of the show, I would feel the faint glimmer of an emotion which I no longer thought I possessed or that had withered to nothing from lack of use: jealousy.

The fog had probably settled in for the rest of the day. I would have to make do with slow progress, regardless of what I wanted. This was my last trip and I wanted to acquit myself in as professional a manner as possible. What else was left? I shouldn't have diverted to Will's and, if I had, as I had to, I should have got back to the normal route rather than satisfying my own whims for a fresh scene. I couldn't see anything anyway.

Sometimes you have to ask yourself why things can't leave you alone: memory; circumstances; other people. You can get by all right if other people don't have plans for you or if you don't feature in plans that people have drawn out for themselves. Being part of a plan like that takes you out of the driving seat.

Being a passenger isn't much like being a driver. Since I became a driver I haven't made a good passenger most of the time. I was a good passenger when I was a kid. In fact I liked it then. I liked to be on the road. Being out meant you were going to experience new things. Sometimes those new things would be imaginative events triggered by what you saw through the car window. Images come and go, get added to the network of ideas already formed in your head. You gather in new information and see how it fits. Passenger travel is a history lesson of road nomenclature, layouts and categories; it's a geography lesson in town and country topography, an education in social structure, architectural development, the sculptural disposition of trees and hedge-lines. All of this seen through every type of weather, from inside the steel and glass cocoon of the moving vehicle. Think how boring it is when the car has stopped, what a relief it is when the car starts again.

You glimpse snapshots of human psychology: arguments between mother and child on dangerous street corners; the weariness of the dray man lowering the last barrel into the pub cellar; the freedom of the postman coming off his shift. In the dark the ever-welcoming lights of the passing homes reveal tableaux of individual family lives, shown for a second and then replaced by the next in a flick-book of humanity.

To me, the road was all about symbols: chevrons; arrows; T's and Y's and crosses; stripes and hatchings; circles; triangles; squares. It had its instructions in curt English, boundaries and limits, denials and permissions, policed by the silent population of cone people, stoically defending no-man's land. The road functioned by a set of clear and unambiguous rules that brought direction out of chaos, fashioned flow out of the requirements of so many million road users.

I sat in the back, savouring the smells of new places that had wafted through the air vents, mixing with the cooked scent of vinyl and dusty carpet. Even a fifteen-minute journey was an experience, delineated by curves and turns, ticked off by the clicking of the indicators.

The green jewel flashed on the dashboard just enough to confirm that it had done its job and I sucked another humbug offered from the infinite supply that resided in the glove box.

Travel has its own time – fast or slow – but always different to the time-frame of the environment through which you are travelling. That separateness gives you the freedom to observe, safe in the fact that you are always moving on, that the risks and predicaments observed through the screen will always be escaped and left behind to be worked through in their own time.

Being on the road is time travel: the metal box takes you through the spatial dimension to some other location, always later, always in a different place. Even if you've been on a round trip, that place has moved on in the infinite vastness of space and you and the place have operated on a slightly different progress of time – Einstein proved that.

These days I have learned the mystery of control. I've moved from the back seat to the front and there's no going back. In the driver's seat there is not the same leisure for casual observation, but what you do see often has a greater weight of meaning. The traffic and road conditions have consequences for your continued existence. You must always keep that in mind as your ton and a quarter exoskeleton cuts through the ether towards your final destination.

CHANGE

I suppose Dave and Terence started behaving oddly about two months before this last trip. Oddly for them, that is. Over the three years the whole thing had become routine. It wasn't even worthy of comment, most of the time. They had seemed happy with the way things were going. Now Dave seemed that little bit more serious. He was still affable enough in my presence, but you could tell he had something else on his mind. He's not bright enough to have two things on his mind without one of them showing at the edges. To me it stuck out a mile.

Terence was simply busier. He was getting out a lot more and looking like he'd lunched. Increasingly, I spent time on the bike, at his behest, dropping off jiffy-bag packages at litter bins in streets all over Greater London. Doing so without looking suspicious is an art in itself, but I usually got around it by wrapping the package in crumpled newspaper and making like it was the remains of a fish dinner. Whether this made things more difficult for the recipient I neither know nor care – Terence didn't forward any complaints.

I have a natural sense for when change is coming on. To me it's as if the energy of the situation is being gradually re-directed. It often happens long before the actual, physical change takes place. I felt it at the end of college. It was obvious, of course, that work and career were going to replace study and academia, but there was something more than that. I also knew on some level that college had been a bottleneck, where all the necessity of decision-making had been suspended until I was past the degree. The supposition was that, by reaching the target, I would be set up for a better life afterwards. In the end, though, I was more adrift than ever.

It's like this final trip. On the road you have to deal with the problems in hand: whether to fill up before getting on the motorway; whether to pass that caravan on this little straight or whether to hope for a better stretch; whether to have chosen a busy trunk road on a foggy day. Looking closely at the detail means you can forego the bigger picture. In fact, for a while you can forget that there's a bigger picture at all.

All business was jiffy-bag business. I needed things to occupy myself. When I wasn't riding for Terence I was riding for the hell of it, networking the streets until I was saddle sore. I didn't care – the very repetitiveness of the process was the key to its mind-numbing benefits. I was like a putative taxi-driver doing The Knowledge, only I wasn't trying to take any of it in. Street names were just clues I needed to find a way when it was time to go home. I kept inside the cranial boundary of the M25. Everything inside it was the London brain and I travelled along its thought routes, trying to make sense. But sense isn't made from a single thought, a single moving point amongst those billions of cells, it's a thought-collective of a million points in a simultaneous motion of concerted effort. I was retracing the same routes like I was retracing the same thoughts: Gail; Dawn; Gail's place; jiffy bags with unknown contents to unknown clients; what Terence was up to.

'I got a job for you,' he said.

'Yeah?'

'Package.'

'Where?'

'Bit further out, Newmarket. You can do that?'

'Of course.'

This was a bigger package – A4 size – heavier.

'Thing is, John, you can't ever let this out of your sight. Keep it on you all the time. You'll take it tomorrow.'

I could see that he meant it. He had all the details on a piece of paper.

'Don't leave the instructions lying around. Don't throw them away.'

'You want me to keep them?'

'Just don't put them in the bin.'

I wondered what he meant by that.'Okay.'

'And when you've done we won't be needing you for a week. Dave'll give you some money.'

I took the package to bed with me, whatever the contents were. A package is just a package until it's opened – they're all the same.

Outside of the M25 I felt unaccountably free. Thought processes were much clearer on the open road. I cruised up the M11 at a steady seventy, enjoying the change from city to suburb to countryside. I didn't let the weight of traffic bother me and, anyway, there wasn't the usual level of cut and thrust. The bike took it all in its stride. The bike always took everything in its stride – one of the benefits of being a mechanism. Beneath my wheels life's undulations rolled away, Harlow, Bishop's Stortford, Saffron Walden, Junction 9 for the A11, dual carriageway, off to the 1034 at Six Mile Bottom. Sometimes the straight road has the best rhythm.

The package was in my shoulder bag, my leathers saw off the headwind, fewer insects splatting off my visor in the rising autumn, mid-October, every mile another mile away from Gail, away from the unit and everything it contained, even if I was spun on a thread of one of Terence's machinations. I throttled up a bit and overtook some slow-moving traffic – not in the van this time, matey, I can have you – watching them fall back into bug-stain reflections in the rear-view mirrors.

Then the game of trying to find the drop-off point: an access road on some corner of a field with a white fence, next to a stand of trees. Terence's instructions were exact, as always. I rode past slowly first to survey the lay of the land. I could see only a kid standing next to a big horse, about twenty yards back from the turn off. I went a mile up the road, turned around and loped back to the spot. The kid was still there. I checked the time and the time was right. Terence wouldn't be wrong about a detail like that. I turned up the lane and cruised to a halt a little way shy of the two figures. I got off, but left the engine running.

The horse looked expensive and the kid was actually a very small man. His face was lined like he'd been hanging on hard to reins for decades in all kinds of weather. I could tell he didn't like the look of me. Perhaps he didn't like bikes, but what was he riding other than a four-legged motorcycle?

I gave it a few seconds and took my helmet off. I looked into the woods in case he wasn't alone. I couldn't see anyone, but I couldn't be conclusive. The little man was approaching me.

'Have you brought the merchandise?'

He was definitely the one, then, 'Yes, I've got it. You alone?'

'Could be, maybe not.'

'Well, hadn't you better decide?' This wasn't fucking international espionage.

'Yes, I'm on my own.'

He'd walked right up to me, now. He could have been thirty-five or sixty. I swung the bag off my shoulder and pulled out the package, 'Now, if I could just have your signature.'

'You what?'

'It's a joke, mate, thought it might lighten the mood.'

I handed the package over. He shook it. What did that tell him? Nothing, I'd shaken it myself.

A rustling from the woods. I looked up quick. Just the horse nuzzling in the undergrowth. Perhaps this *was* international espionage.

'All right,' I said, 'That's it, I'm off.'

He was off too, on his fiery steed. I saw him in the distance, charging across the field to whomever was waiting for the package. Knowing these things wasn't part of my job description.

Only I knew that Gail had left her back door open. It had taken me an hour and a half of sitting on her wall, looking into the empty rooms after she had gone out, but it had become obvious that the door to the garden was slightly ajar.

The balmy afternoon had turned into a balmy evening: the autumn of existence. After I'd got back from Newmarket I had the rest of the evening to myself. So I went home, waited until it was dark, changed out of my leathers into the combat jacket and camouflage trousers that I wore for operations these days and made my way by the familiar route to Gail's garden. After she had gone out I'd stayed. I don't know why. Fatigue maybe – I hadn't been still all day.

I knew she was going out for some time. She was dressed for an evening out, not just a quick trip to the shops. I stayed away from the wind, hidden in the thickness of the tree fronds in as dark a place as one could expect to find. I pulled up my collar and closed my eyes for a while, then couldn't get comfortable and went back to survey the land.

The door was definitely ajar, just slightly, but enough to be certain that it was not properly shut, so of course it was not locked. Without even thinking about it I stepped down from the wall. The only sound I made was the merest rustling as I passed between the branches, lost in the breeze. For the first time I stood on her ground. The sensation was palpable.

I stayed in the shadow of the trees, checking for signs of life in the upstairs windows of the adjacent houses. I walked slowly, around the perimeter of the garden, making myself a fluid pouring imperceptibly towards her door. Nearer the door the light was stronger. I was inside quickly with the door shut behind me.

I hadn't thought anything through. I hadn't even considered the idea of being inside. I was unprepared for what was supposed to happen next. I stayed in the kitchen, backed onto the door, casting no shadows for anyone looking in.

The kitchen was quite small, but neatly arranged: uncluttered granite worktops; two chairs and a small table; a notice board with postcards pinned to it; a phone on the wall; a metal grid holding hooks suspending kitchen implements; her last used coffee mug left by the sink.

I went through to the dining area, quietly, trying not to make shapes in the shadows. Not even the ticking of a clock. The air was thick and unreal. I was in it, pulling in the evidence at close hand. I stood by her big dining table, started to reach towards the surface, where I'd seen her eat her meal, stopped myself. It was impossible to touch anything here. I could see that there were shelves of books and ornaments invisible from the garden. I pieced together the evidence of what I had seen with what I now knew to be true. I looked out into the garden, looking for where I was sitting, made my way silently through to the living room.

The print above the fireplace, glimpsed through the front window, was a Turner skyscape, not an abstract. On the mantelpiece was a picture of a woman I didn't recognise. No mirror. An award of some sort. The suite looked comfortable. I looked for her shape, impressed in the upholstery. I bent down carefully in the slight glow of the hall light. Where was she? I'd be less obvious upstairs.

The mirror was in the hall. Her green jacket hung on its hanger from one of a row of pegs. Another coat I hadn't seen: a winter coat? Underneath the stairs I could see the door to a cupboard. I looked at the doorway, trying to estimate the size of the space inside. Something was forming in my consciousness. I backed off to stop it, took a breath. It was too light in the hall for my liking, far too near to the street. Time to move on. I drifted upstairs, like smoke.

I arrived on the landing as if in an alien world. The atmosphere was breathable, but not the consistency of the air to which I was accustomed. I closed my eyes and tried to recall the smell of Bridget's house. Smells are most evocative. I could not invoke. I could smell the shampoo she'd used to wash her hair before she went out.

Four doors – three open, no sound. The bathroom, still slightly steamy – I prevented myself from entering. Her bedroom.

A large T-shirt lay on the bed: her nightdress. A double bed with one pillow in the middle; her alarm clock by the bedside table; a ceramic frog; some fragrance more familiar. I stood in the silence, almost breathing, trying to discern. Something had happened to the normal way that time was supposed to work. I'd stepped into a vortex of temporal fluctuations. Her clothes were hidden in the wardrobe, in drawers. I was incapable of opening them. The room resonated.

I stepped back out to the landing. The only other open door was the mystery room at the back of the house. I went in there. I was right, it was an office.

An L-shaped desk occupied most of the room, a filing cabinet and wall-to-wall shelving the rest. I could feel her presence here even stronger than the bedroom. The downstairs rooms had a public feel to them; up here was her private space. I could almost feel her in here. The computer on the desk was switched off, but it would contain lists of her contacts, saved e-mails from friends and colleagues, a recent history of what she'd been browsing on the net. The books on her shelves were a catalogue of her interests. I could enter into her existence through the portal of this office. I looked down the shelves, reading off the titles: a number of dictionaries, a thesaurus, books on geology and geography that could have been her college textbooks, a book on birds, a few books on the use of language, a large-scale motoring atlas of the British Isles and a spiral-bound A-Z of London. On a shelf by itself a digital radio, then a shelf with a few knick-knacks: another photograph of someone I didn't recognise; a Moorcroft vase; a cigar-shaped pebble with a hole in one end.

I left the house quickly. The feeling of floating had gone. I could hear every creak of the floorboards on the way down the stairs, the water in the central heating pipes, the ticking of the kitchen clock. I could hear my own, short, sharp breaths and feel the cold in my hands and feet from sitting on the wall.

SHADOW

I took a once-only shipment of eight cases over to New Cross. Dave came with me. It was like a Mexican stand-off: I stood with Dave, our backs to the van, parked up on the top floor of a multi-storey car park. Two blokes drove up in a Lexus and parked up in a space opposite. They got out and we all stood and stared at each other for five minutes. Dave spent the time spinning his signet ring around on his finger – I could just see him out of the corner of my eye. After the time was up Dave stepped out and met one of the blokes on the neutral ground between our cars. Half of me wanted to laugh – I'd seen it all a million times on television and in film. They exchanged a few words, which drifted away on the wind, and Dave came back and told me to unload the boxes onto the deck. He looked chuffed, but I could see the anxiety underlying it.

Six weeks before the final trip. Dave never said what it was about. Neither of them let on whether there was any money in it and, on this occasion, I didn't even get a bonus. Still, it had made a hole in an otherwise boring day.

Afterwards, I dropped Dave back at the unit and sat for a while looking at my reflection in the rear-view mirror. My teeth were clenched so much that my jaw muscles were bulging. My eyes were stones. John had gone one stop further down a one-way road.

I went into the unit and chucked the van keys back to Dave. He took them without a word and went in to talk to Terence. I followed.

He started to talk to Terence, but shut up when Terence nodded to him to signal my presence. They looked like strangers.

'You want something?' said Dave.

'You finished with me?'

'Yeah, Tuesday.'

The flow of energy had changed. It was a similar feeling to that when we first set up the route, only with none of the enthusiasm.

I went round on Tuesday, ready for another bin drop. There were people without names hanging around the unit. One of them looked a bit like Dave, could even have been his brother, but there are enough short-cropped, thick-set men around for them to be a sub-species of their own. There was a tall guy in a long leather coat that must have cost the best part of a grand and two blokes smoking Marlboro Lights and discussing the merits of Terence & Dave's entertainment set-up. I could feel a definite air of new business.

The no-namers didn't pay me much heed. Dave seemed surprised to see me.

'What are you doing?' he said.

'Tuesday.'

'Yeah, er…'

Now Terence had appeared, 'Yeah, John, you're not going to be needed.'

'No?'

'Not today. Dave'll give you something for your trouble.'

I didn't give it too much thought, especially with an extra two hundred quid in my pocket for what was essentially a trip in to work and back. It hadn't even been that busy on the road. Then I started to wonder why Dave would make a mistake like that. It kept my mind occupied while I sat on Gail's wall on a particularly cold night.

Then I started seeing Specca about. The first time it could have been a simple coincidence: he was there when I came out of one of my favourite bars. He acted like he hadn't seen me and ducked into a newsagent's. The second time, I was coming back from the unit on the way to my flat. He got so close to me in his car that I could hear his clapped-out engine even through the sides of my helmet. If he was going to follow me he would have to do better than that – I simply transferred onto the M4 and headed west. When it was clear enough I opened her up. Gallantly his bag of nails tried to keep up, farting blue smoke out of the back, but he stood no chance. A couple of junctions later I slipped off and came back into town on the A4, imagining him driving all the way to Bristol on his fool's errand.

I thought I caught him a couple more times over the

next week, but I was either wrong or he was getting better at it. The last time, though, there was no doubt. I had just dropped at Daventry and he was two cars back as I drove onto the estate. This time he was in a red Carlton, but it was definitely him – you don't get two people who look like Specca.

That really got me thinking. It got me thinking a lot. Perhaps I should have told Terence and Dave, but in the end I didn't. They had secrets and, at the time, it felt better that I should have some of my own.

I had the rest of that trip to think it over. I didn't see Specca again. Probably I was getting too far from home. These people are all metropolitan people: they think it's all cows and pit heaps north of Watford. They don't go there unless they have to. Not that it prevented me looking over my shoulder all the way round. If it wasn't him, I figured, it was going to be some other agent. Consequently, I suspected everyone. Funny what it does to you when you think you're being watched. You're trying to listen all the time, like they'll give themselves away in a whispered snatch of conversation. It's perhaps something to do with race memories of being crept up upon by predators: you're always alert to the crack of a twig or a deep rush of breath over bared teeth.

I also kept an eye out for vehicles following the van. That was stupid. There are always people who you will see again and again on a long trip. You may pass them, they pass you, you re-pass them when they're having their break and they re-pass you later trying to make up time. Sometimes you can travel two hundred miles within two hundred yards of another van. They might just turn off onto another route or they might drop at another unit in the same business park that you are going to. That's the nature of the road.

Regardless, I spent the whole of the trip misdirecting my attention when I should have been concentrating on the road, wondering whether I was as alone as I wanted to be.

It even affected my time with Dawn. I was even more outspoken about the other John and I had to go down to the garage twice in a sleepless night to check the contents of the van.

So now I was paranoid and deprived of sleep. I got started late and drank too much coffee in an attempt at kick-starting the senses. The whole thing turned into a blinding rush in which everyone else on the road was intent on getting in my way.

Then, coming out of North Shields, I ran into trouble. A twat in a maroon 306 pulled out of a side street directly into my path. I could see he wasn't going to stop – there was no way he could have done. I could see the fear on his girlfriend's face as he came out from the left. For a moment I wondered how she could be pointing at me and driving at the same time, then realised that it must be left-hand drive, even though the number plate was British. I sounded my horn. If I hadn't had my wits about me I would have run straight into them. I sounded the horn long, because it was merited with driving like that. He went another fifty yards and pulled an emergency stop. I put my right foot through the floor trying to avoid the shunt. He came to a complete halt and remained.

There is another type of driver on the list, luckily far rarer than any of the other types: The Insane. You can go weeks or months or years without actually coming across one, though it's my contention that they're a species on the increase. The Insane aren't just mad on the road, they're mad in everything they do. They'll be mad at home, making life hell for their neighbours; they'll be mad when they're out drinking in town on a Saturday night, which is why the Police have taken to wearing body armour. They might not be officially, clinically insane, but their actions and reactions don't conform to anyone's normal standards of social behaviour. I've wondered what can possibly be going through their minds as they overtake a column of wagons on the hard shoulder in amongst blinding spray. I've tried to make sense of the carnage when one of them has sped the wrong way down a dual carriageway to in an attempt to escape the law. They'll rocket through the countryside in columns on overpowered bikes overtaking everything until the last one in the convoy comes a cropper trying to keep up with his mates, though I might concede that this is a temporary, summer madness or some collective nonsense that takes over under group conditions.

Even though they are a comparatively rare occurrence,

whenever you are on the road you must always keep a weather eye open for the Insane. They can overtake into you on the wrong side of the road, misjudge it and drop on to you from the bridge above your carriageway, they will, inevitably, pull out on you every time without looking and, every time, make an incident over what could have remained a minor indiscretion.

I could see them arguing – a really heated exchange with hand signals. Fuck it, I thought, I can't sit here. I pulled out wide and passed him, even though we were at the top of a descent on a tight left-hander, much to the consternation of a driver coming the other way who must have thought I was out of my mind overtaking on a blind summit. I went on my way.

Next thing he's hard on my bumper, close enough for me to see in detail in my rear-view mirror. She is actually punching him in the side of the head, while he's pushing at her face, trying to fend her off. It's crazy, because he's driving like an acrobat while having a full on fistfight with his passenger.

I can see what she's thinking: that he's almost killed them both. Certainly, if I'd have T-boned them I would have gone into her side of the car. Now that I think about it I bet he didn't even look. Then I think that he's trying to scare her with his driving because this is an argument that goes back before he pulled out.

He backs off a touch, still grappling at her and I think that it's all over, but right then he pulls out and overtakes me. I can see his stupid face as he goes past, making some ludicrous point that defies logic. He cuts me up. There's barely six inches between us. Then my foot's through the floor for a second time. I don't even have time to disengage the clutch properly and I'm stalled. He gets out and comes towards me, bouncing on rigid legs. His fists are stones. Someone else has come up behind and blocked my escape.

Some people are born to rage, all dark eyebrows and deep-set, popping eyes, look like they wake up and hammer their way through breakfast.

For a moment I think that I might keep the window wound up and sit it out, but the caffeine and paranoia won't let me, so I reach under my seat and get out.

The thing about the angry bounce is that it's a slow way to travel. All the energy's directed up and down. He would be better off running over, doing what he's got to do and running back. As it is the guy behind me has found a way to get off my bumper and got past.

He's still coming. He can see me – the focus of all his pain and anguish at having cut me up in his poxy rep box. He seems to have been bearing down on me forever, though it's only been a second. With him comes the caustic retch of adrenaline, the sum of all his hatred, bile and resentment.

It strikes me that I shouldn't be out here facing down someone so obviously quick to violence, who explodes at the sounding of a horn. It strikes me that he looks like he may have boxed. I strike him with the wheel brace I've had hidden in my hand behind the van door. He drops like a bag of sugar, his red rage a collapsed heap on the crown of the road.

I'm not going to wait. I drive round him in the van as he struggles to his feet.

What the hell was I thinking? John's employed because he's cool, he gets the job done. Any number of people have a mobile phone and could have called the Police. The Police could have driven past right then. They have a happy knack of doing that. I looked back on the load and tried to calm my breath.

I kept to the speed limits and stopped worrying about the time. If I was late getting to Motherwell, Bill wouldn't mind. Specca was just doing a bit of industrial espionage. We were in business after all. Business is competitive. Something was changing in our business so Specca's lot might fancy picking up our business if they could find out who our contacts were. Simple as that.

Our business was winding down. Dave and Terence were moving onto something else. Perhaps they were going fully legit. One part of the business is slowing down, while another is bubbling away in the crucible of preparation. Perhaps leather coat and his mates are going to take over the old part and free up T and D for whatever's coming up for them. The worst thing that's going to happen is that I'm going to be out of a job. So what? I've done it to the best of my ability while it lasted and I've made enough money to tide me over for a bit. In a way it would be better if I left all this stuff behind anyway, if only for peace of mind.

I kept on telling myself these things as I completed the trip. By the time I got back I had it all sorted out in my head. The road can do that for you. You know how long you've got and, in a way, you can drive yourself towards a conclusion. I was even quite happy about it. Then, three days later, I was out on the bike and I saw Specca again, with another man, in his red Carlton. After that I was so confused I didn't know whether to think up or down.

CANVEY

Someone had nicked my rubbish. I knew this, because it wasn't yet bin day and I'd taken some more stuff down to add to the bag only to find it gone. My neighbours' bags remained. It had happened in the night because I had only put the bag out the previous evening. I looked around to see if I could see any suspicious looking faces but, of course, there weren't – who steals your bin bag and then sits around for hours waiting to see your reaction?

There wasn't anything in it for anyone to see. There would be no correspondence, no utility bills, no photographs or paperwork or receipts other than those from the supermarket, for which I wasn't even registered for a loyalty card. There would be bottles and cans and the waste from my food preparation, including the chicken carcass from last week's two-day roast dinner marathon. They would enjoy finding that.

I wondered whether this might become a regular event. Perhaps I should take to placing things deliberately in my rubbish as red herrings. I could borrow someone else's bills and receipts, make up some fatuous correspondence and throw that away, having first ripped it into small pieces so that they would have to spend hours putting the food-stained fragments back together. I could copy out some intrigue from a spy novel or something and see if they could make the literary connection. I could put in some of your actual red herrings – nothing stinks as much as rotting fish.

Afterwards I felt slightly violated. I didn't want anyone looking through my stuff, even if it was only the stuff I was throwing away. It was still something connected with my private existence.

I could still catch Specca on the odd day. I never knew when to expect him. Sometimes it was possible that he'd got away with watching me, but he didn't really have a clue about zones.

I'm a good driver because I'm observant. My Zone Two is continually adapting to the prevailing road conditions, to all those vagaries of topography and climate. Like the rally driver, part of my attention might be focussed two miles up the road, at a stretch of tarmac that I'm not going to get to for two or three minutes. So, when I get there, there aren't going to be any significant surprises, because I've already assessed the general layout and the likely hazards. If there's an obstacle up ahead I already know about it.

I do this when I'm out walking on city streets. I don't walk around in a daze with my head down, I'm looking about. I watch for people and I watch for traffic. I look for possible risks in the distance and take steps to avoid them.

Specca couldn't be a very good driver; he was always

getting into my Zone Two. He would think he was staying out of sight behind the last corner, but I would always be able to catch his reflection in the windows of passing cars or I would turn a corner myself and see him briefly in the periphery of my vision as I changed direction. I was looking out for him, so my Zone Two was going to be at least as big as his. Unless he was watching me through binoculars from some building, which I thought was unlikely, I should probably be able to spot him every time.

However, it was still making it difficult to see Gail. I didn't mind Specca trailing me down to the unit, he always turned off before the last junction anyway, but there was no way I wanted him to be getting in the way of my expeditions. I took him on a long walk.

I waited until I was sure he was following me and strode around for three-quarters of an hour taking every turn I could. I bought a day pass, got on the tube and performed a random circuit of the Circle Line. Every so often I'd get off at a station, go up to the street, wander aimlessly for a while, pop into one or two shops for a browse, come out and go back down to the line. Sometimes I tried to make myself look furtive, so that he might think I was up to something, then I'd take some time waiting at a café table with some refreshment, knowing that he wouldn't be able to refresh himself in case he missed something or I made a sudden move. On the tube I made it relatively easy for him. I didn't rush for the train or dither at the platform edge as if I wasn't going to get on. I telegraphed when I was going to get off by getting up and standing near the door. We kept this up for hours. He was so assiduous that I figured he must be under some heavy-duty orders: 'Follow that John and make sure you don't lose him.'

I lost him, just like they do in the films. I got onto a train and, right at the last moment, without any prior indication, I got off again. The doors shut on him and I was sprinting up the exit stairs of the station closest to Gail's place of work.

She came out right on time, not too long after she must have come off the air, time enough for a wind-down and a debriefing. She was dressed casual/smart – good for radio if she was going to get captured on their web cam. I tried to think when I had ever not seen her looking good, even after drinking late with me and falling into bed. Even with the shiny patina of sleep and hair like a nest she looked great.

I followed her through the streets, even though I'd been on my feet all afternoon driving Specca around. She was easy to follow. I was in the swing of it.

I followed her to a café and waited outside while she drank a cup of coffee and ate a cake. She took twenty-four minutes – must have been a hard day's broadcasting, though I hadn't been able to listen. Now it was dark and she probably wanted a moment's readjustment before she went home for the night. When she went, I would be outside until she decided it was time to turn in.

It was easy to follow her onto the tube: my day pass gave me access to all zones. We made our way majestically across the city, sometimes riding, sometimes walking, to our mutual destination.

I watched her lean back into the settee and close her eyes. My eyes were open to it. Wherever she was, she was mine. I would never enter her house again without an invitation, but I would always be there.

She prepared and ate some pasta. She finished off the remainder of a bottle of wine and went up to her office room. I felt bad for her, in some way, that she should be alone on a dark night in the dying fall. One shouldn't face winter alone. I didn't want her to be seeing the man again, but I didn't like to think that she was lonely. She was too special for that.

I left when there were no more lights on and got a cab back to my place. There was no sign of Specca. I drew all the curtains and sat in the darkness with a glass of brandy, listening to a message from Dave on my answer machine saying that they were going to be needing me for something in a couple of days, though it wasn't yet time to be going out on the route. When I'd finished my brandy I looked through a chink in the curtains until I was satisfied that there was no one out there with me on their mind, rechecked the door, went to bed and tried to dream nice thoughts.

The next day he was back. If he wanted me to I could take him for another ride. Perhaps I should take a rest day and bore him rigid. I could think of the most uncomfortable place possible. Somewhere within the boundary of the M25 there must be a place where I could set myself up in the utmost comfort while he shivered out in the cold or got wet or deafened or something, preferably all three. I could wander around and drive him to distraction.

I had a leisurely breakfast at home. I slobbed around for a bit. I ate a leisurely lunch and slobbed around a bit more before, finally, I thought, why not? Lead him a happy dance, lose him once more. I wanted to see Gail again. I was longing to see her. I got out the one photograph of her that I had in my possession and tried to read things into it. She stayed enigmatic. I hadn't taken the photograph. I couldn't remember who had. I didn't really know the context.

By mid afternoon I was showered and ready. I thought I might take the Metropolitan Line all the way out to Amersham. I could have an envelope in my hand which I could drop into someone's, anyone's letterbox. That would get them thinking. I might see some interesting things on the way out. I'd never travelled right out to the end of a line. I could take all afternoon, lose him and go and see what Gail was up to.

I set off walking. Specca wasn't far behind. I wondered if he'd got a bollocking for losing me. I certainly hoped so. I kept the walking up for the best part of an hour. At one point I bought a notebook, scribbled some nonsense on a page, tore it out and sealed it into an envelope. I sat on a bench at a bus stop so it was clear what I was doing. I headed for my chosen station.

Specca's outfit deserved all the complications they could get. I should create a whole artificial business with contacts, drops, packages, premises even, and fuck up their intelligence system. That would teach them to send out a cunt like Specca to go stalking me...

I stopped in the middle of the street, unsteady on my feet. Sometimes your own stupidity is too staggering to comprehend. What was the difference? If he was stalking me, I was stalking Gail. I was a stalker. It hadn't occurred to me once. Worse than that, I was a celebrity stalker, a pathetic figure of tabloid ridicule, a no-hoper living in a fantasyland of connection and attraction. I propped myself up against a lamppost. Why had it taken me until I had my own stalker to realise what I was? Specca was stalking me was stalking Gail. He was probably being stalked as well. There's probably a whole column of stalkers, all following each other about like a queue of traffic, trailing back into the infinite distance. There were probably people setting off from home at all times of the day and night so that they could join their place on the stalking queue. Maybe I was stalking Gail and she was stalking the last person on the queue stalking me, like a giant ouroboros or the M25, everyone going round, nose to tail, for fucking ever, to end up where they started only further on in time, closer to death but no further forward.

I couldn't see Gail again. I was putting her at risk. If it

wasn't Specca behind me it might be someone else I didn't recognise. That might already have happened. How could I have done this? I needed to find a bar and I needed a drink. In fact I needed to drink until I didn't have the capacity for any more. Let Specca sit outside and wait.

The wheels of the bike turned beneath me. I chose the most tortuous route possible to get out to Hemel Hempstead. If there was anyone trying to follow me they were going to have a hard time. Even on a bike they would find it hard. I hitched onto the A41 and blasted when I could. Who's going to be able to keep up at a hundred and thirty? I left the main road abruptly at Tring and cut down through Bucks. until there was no one with me at all. I parked up in a dark corner and waited for the sun to go down before I cranked her up again and made a similarly tortuous journey back into town. I was ready on Gail's wall before she was home.

It was cold, but at least it was dry and still. I was certain that no one knew I was here. This was the last time. There had to be a last time and, if that was the case, then I wanted to know that it was from the outset, not to find out that we'd had our last time after the fact.

I had the photograph in my pocket. She had come home, but she was taking a long time in the office upstairs. I needed a leak, but I was careful to let it out into the garden behind, as quietly as possible. I sat and waited, into the night, in the way that stalkers do, all their energy focussed on the object of their desire, all thoughts a mismatch of fantasy and reality. If this was the last time, I wanted her to spend some time in the kitchen or at the dining table so that I could see her before I resigned from being a stalker and went back to being a common criminal. Yet she wasn't having it. She'd been a bit late getting back, so I guessed she must have eaten on the way. She was probably going to spend the whole night working on her computer and then she'd go straight to bed. Maybe I didn't have the stamina for this – I shouldn't have spent all that time getting drunk the night before, trying Specca's patience while he waited outside. I'd had a worse hangover than I could ever remember, which even the bike trip hadn't fully blown away. I looked up to the faint glow coming through the office curtains and watched and waited and waited.

Light fell into the garden, a thick wedge of light from the kitchen door. I hadn't really been paying attention. There was too much going on inside of me to be able to keep a perfect watch all the time. The upstairs light was still on. Now the kitchen light had come on and the door had been opened. The patch of light yawned and the sound formed a figure. She was lit from one side. You could see the contrast was too much for her. She closed the door behind her and stepped forward into the dark.

I stayed still. I was in the best position. I'd never seen her out the back, but then I'd never been here in daylight. What was she doing out in the dark?

She stood still for a moment, as if she was listening for something. She looked left and right and then, slowly, walked forwards, towards the back of the garden. I was transfixed. She came towards me, away from the white light of the kitchen window and into the blue glow of the night. I crouched on the wall like a gargoyle. My head was in amongst the green fronds of the trees, just in the shadow. She continued, not just to the limit of the lawn, but right towards me. How did she know? I couldn't be seen. She came right up to the tree line and stopped. What was she thinking? I could see her so clearly, even in the half-light. She looked as she looked on that first night at the crêperie, afterwards, when I walked her home. She looked exactly as she did before everything happened, when everything was a promise and not, for better or worse, a historical fact. She stood quite still and looked into the shadow of my face. She looked sad, as if something that she needed had been put forever out of her reach. We were alone together in the garden. She must know something. She must have been able to sense something with her magic powers.

She reached out and brushed the leaves with her fingers. She looked down momentarily and started to turn. I could reach out to her. I could raise my hand and bring it out into the light. I could step down from the wall and make myself clear. From here she was close enough for me to touch with my outstretched hand but, of course, I could not – she stood on the other side of an impossible, impossible divide, measured in centimetres.

I was in Bridget's car. Gail was in the front, but I'd been given the whole of the back seat to myself as compensation. I was wearing a new dark suit. I'd had a special close shave and put on some after-shave lotion I'd bought especially for the occasion. Bridget was asking for directions and Gail was providing them. She even knew where there were likely to be hold-ups and road works. I was content to be free of the responsibility. No doubt there would be nice food and drink at the wedding reception and the clement weather would make it a pleasure for everyone.

Gail turned round and asked me if I was all right and I said I was fine. In fact, I was more than fine: Bridget was looking good in her wedding outfit, but I would be with the best looking girl at the ceremony. I didn't mind if everyone wanted to look as long as they understood that she was with me. I straightened my tie and prepared to enjoy the ride.

The daylight was cold and I'd been woken by spots of dew from the trees. My eyes were glued together with something. I started to yawn and then stifled myself, because it was obvious that I'd fallen asleep in Gail's garden. I was slumped in the corner beneath the trees. I'd only gone there for a moment to take a rest. Now it was morning, probably well into he morning, and there was no cover of darkness. Too tired and too hungover – I knew I was losing it. I drew my legs in as far as I could. How much cover had I got?

I found my way to my feet and tried to take stock. There was no denying that I'd fucked up, big time. I got back on the wall and tried to manoeuvre myself round to my usual vantage point. There was no sign of life in the house. I checked my watch. She must have already gone out and, fuck, I was supposed to be down at the unit for a job. I took one last look at the garden, regretted that I couldn't spend more time, because it was the first time I'd seen it in daylight and it was the last time I was ever going to see it. Then I traversed the wall into the next garden.

The whole escapade was much more exposed in daylight. What I'd thought was good cover turned out to laughably inadequate. I was lucky that it was too cold for people to be out, except for the third house along where, in my rush, I dropped straight off the wall in front of a bloke with a lawn rake.

'What the hell?' he said.

'Sorry,' I said, 'just came to get my ball back.'

'You…'

'Can't stop to chat.' I shot around him and headed for the next garden. There was no point trying to be secretive now. I had to get out and get on the bike fast and get out of here. I had to get to the unit.

Dave gave me a package and told me to drop it at an

address in Canvey Island. When it was done I had to phone him up and say. He fished around in his pocket and handed over five hundred pounds, just for that.

'Take your girlfriend out,' he said.

It took me the rest of the day. I got snarled up in the worst traffic in living history trying to get to the A13 and then nearly ran out of fuel overtaking a convoy of rides from a funfair. The last thing you want is the bike cutting out two thirds of the way past a waltzer with a Range Rover hurtling at you from the opposite direction. It felt just like the old days.

After Canvey I shot up to Chelmsford and ate in the most expensive place I could get into looking like I did. I even bought a couple of shots of hugely inflated Armagnac from the connoisseurs' list and sipped them slowly while the waiters watched their watches.

There was something wrong with me. I sat there and tried to map it. But maps are a lie. They show roads out of scale and simplify the landscape. There are places on the Atlas of Britain that are empty space: Watton to Mundford in East Anglia, Sunk Island on the north bank of the Humber, Goole Wastes and whole sections of Scotland above the 836 and 839.

That's how I felt, sitting there looking at myself: like I was staring into empty space.

I had to leave the bike and take a late train home. Public transport's all right as it goes, but not if you're going to have to trail your way back the next day hoping that the bike hasn't been pinched before you get there. I changed carriage twice trying to avoid the drunks, only to have a smart looking woman change hers to avoid a greasy biker twat like me. There was a message in it somewhere, but not one I felt I could get my head around just at that moment. I was obviously an idiot. If I'd had any sense I would have checked into a hotel for the night and saved all the hassle. It would probably have been cheaper. Naturally, the thought had occurred to me about three seconds after the train had left the platform, so I had to spend the journey back metaphorically kicking myself whilst ennui slurred past behind the night black windows.

All I knew was that there was something I didn't know, and I didn't know how to go about finding out.

SPECCA

I was sitting quietly in the van, in a lay-by on the A417 the other side of Ledbury. The phone had just rung. I had heard it, for the first time, chirruping merrily amongst the clothes in my overnight bag. For a while I didn't even realise what it was.

It was Dave. 'All right, John,' he said.

'Yeah, yes.'

'Where you at, then?'

'Gloucester.'

'On schedule then, yeah?'

'Just about.'

'Nice.'

He sounded like a friend. Friends sound friendly, as if they're concerned for your wellbeing.

'So, we'll be seeing you in a couple of hours, yeah?'

'Should be about right.'

We both knew it would be longer than that, but what are a couple of hours between friends? They'd be there when I got back. They always were. They'd probably have one of their favourite videos on to pass the time. It could be *Casino* or *The Big Sleep*.

'See you then,' he said.

I turned the engine off and sat in silence for a while,

watching the weather. A cold wind was beginning to clear the fog.

Where was I? I couldn't be too far off Gloucester, so at least that wasn't too much of a lie. The 417 was a new road to me, but it had hardly registered. For the last hour I had been driving on autopilot. Maybe it was more than an hour. Maybe it was half an hour. Perhaps I'd lost a day without noticing. I knew I was hungry, so I couldn't have eaten anything. Not like John to miss a meal.

There wasn't much for me to do building up to this last trip. There were no more jiffy bags to take out, no more one-off deliveries. I kept myself to myself and thought about the next time I might see Dawn. That got me thinking about Gail, which in turn got me trying to make mental connections. Mostly, though, I tried not to think about anything, using Armagnac as the medium of obliteration. Even so, stuff kept popping into my head when I hadn't asked it to, to the point of having to go to through all of my books a second time in a vain attempt to see if there were any more secret photographs.

Even getting out on the bike didn't seem to help: wherever I was I seemed to take my head with me. One day I did a full circuit of the M25 to see if that would occupy my mind. I just came back pissed off and misanthropic.

So, I was pleased when I got the word from Dave that they wanted me to go down to the unit. Just two weeks after the penultimate tour. I asked whether they were ready for another one, but he said 'No'. Shame, because

Dawn might have been able to take my mind off things for a while.

The weather was bright for the time of year and it was fine out on the bike. I even opened her up when I shouldn't have done, just to feel the thrill. Then, when I got there, Specca's car was parked outside.

The big shutter door was almost closed and I had to bend right down to get underneath it. Why did they want me on such short notice?

They were in Dave's office: Dave and Terence and Specca in Dave's swivel chair. Tied into his swivel chair.

He had something in his mouth that prevented him from speaking. Dave was round the back of the chair, apparently with a grip on his wrists, swivelling the chair to the left and right in slow, mesmeric motion. He looked up at me, 'Oh, hello John. Look Speccy-boy, John's come to see you. You like John, don't you?'

That obviously amused Dave, because he was smiling at Terence.

Terence was smiling himself, though it didn't show on his face.

Dave continued, 'Yeah, you like John so much you thought you'd spend some time with him, didn't you?'

There was only one of him, strapped to the chair with Dave at his back and the bulk of Terence above him. Now there was me on the other side and he was boxed in.

'Had your nose in the trough, haven't you? Been

sticking your nose where it don't belong. Now what happens?' He gave Specca a cuff round the head that hurt me. 'See, John, he likes you.'

If they were going to beat him up I didn't want to see. I didn't like him much – he'd been bothering me recently, but I didn't want to see him beaten black and blue when he wasn't able to defend himself. I turned and went to leave.

'Oh no,' said Dave, 'you've got see this.'

When I looked again Terence had moved. There was something in his hand: the big screwdriver we used when we wanted to get the staples out of cases.

Its flat tip impacted first just behind Specca's left ear. I could see him screaming, but no noise passed his gag. A trickle of blood ran down his neck. Terence tried again, closer to his crown. He used a lot of force, but the blow was misdirected and the tip ran a gouge across the top of his head.

Dave was saying something like, 'You fucking cunt, you nosy fucking cunt.'

Terence didn't like what was going on. He started to jab wildly at Specca's head, each thrust coming faster than the last.

I knew what they were doing. I'd seen *Goodfellas,* where Tommy and Jimmy execute Morrie with an ice pick when they think he's giving the game away. I knew that Terence and Dave thought of themselves as some sort of romanticised gangster types. I wanted to tell them that the skull is thinnest under the occiput, but I couldn't say anything, and Terence found out his own way and got it in.

Specca's eyes were wide behind his glasses. The thick lenses filled with their whites and the deep chasms of his dilated pupils. The eyes stared directly at me, as if to say, 'I have something in mind.'

I laughed – a short, shy, aspirant breath, shy because it knows it's out of place.

The message in Specca's eyes changed. He started to look hard to his left, as if there was something he could find if he could only see far enough around. Then he looked at nothing.

But Terence was looking. He held Specca's head in his hands. He was looking at me. It said it all: how long he'd been waiting to do this to someone, how the business was going to expand at the expense of the competition and how, sometime – soon, but not quite yet – he would be doing this to me. It wasn't a threat, it was an IOU waiting to be cashed. Whatever he told me in words meant nothing compared to the promise in his eyes.

John sat for a long time in the lay-by with the phone still in his hand, re-running the film for the benefit of his mind's eye until, presently, he remembered he had a job to do and drove off.

BRISTOL

I can't remember how I got to Gloucester – the road just seemed to pass away. I was aware only that I hadn't had anything to eat and felt increasingly light and hollow, as if I was gradually being eaten away from the inside. When the process was complete I would be nothing more than a skin operating the controls. The skin would thin and thin again, until it could be seen through, and then hardly seen at all. At the end there would be nothing but an idea of where I had been.

The flux of time and distance is all a product of the mind: it comes and goes according to how it is perceived. In the van you see it coming in by the windscreen and leaving by the back. That's the surface of it. Below the surface the flux forgets the rules, because past time will insist on coming through. It comes up from behind and shoots straight through you.

Past time is measured out in done-journeys, of which there are many types, from the rising arc of school and education, through work and so-called 'informed choice' to the slow debasement of a life for which you had high hopes.

Past time has set into sculpture. When you were close to it you could view it from any angle. As you get further away you can only see it from the one as it recedes into the distance. Yet you still try and recapture the angles and see if the view can be improved. Sometimes it can be forgotten about; sometimes it won't leave you alone.

I wasn't called back down to the unit until it was time for the last trip, two weeks after we had seen Specca off. Each day was a week in itself. For a while he was all I could see, him and Dave and Terence like waxworks cast into a position of demonstration. 'This was how it was done,' the tableau said. I was the only object capable of motion. I could move in any direction, even off the ground but, however far I moved, I could never get them out of sight.

I drank myself fractious. My head ached from dehydration. Even in the warmth of the flat I felt cold. I was either too pissed or too hungover to get out on the bike. Twice I went out to a phone box to make the call; twice I turned back before I was even half way. That confused me more. What was my duty? There was too much to think about – so much that it was spilling out of my head.

Then there was Gail. I had managed to pass years without having to think about her. All that stuff belonged to someone else. Now she had to reappear at the tail end of things, pop up like a ghost and disturb my train of thought, glimmer in the darkness for a moment – enough time to change everything once again – and then be forever out of reach. Now I should be able to put her behind me again, but I couldn't. I put it down to the drink. Then, I'd be out for a walk and I'd keep thinking that I'd seen her. It would just be glimpse of someone's hair or a green jacket and, of course, it was never her, but that didn't do anything to make it less disconcerting.

I must have looked odd, for half the time I was looking over my shoulder for Specca in his beat-up old Granada, expecting him at any minute to be crawling by the curbside ten steps behind. That was my reality, more real than the houses and pavements and street furniture, more real than anything that was going to happen to my friend John in the fullness of time.

The A40 reconnects with the A417 and puts you on to the M5, a road I used to think of as the holiday route, but now just think of as busy. I joined the throng and headed south-west.

Three days before the trip I felt suddenly calm. I took out the picture of Gail and looked closely into it. She was definitely real. I looked at her until there was nothing more to be seen and went off to clean up the flat. I washed up any stuff that was lying around; I laundered all my clothes, folded them up and put them away. I spent an afternoon polishing the bike. Then I was set. I stopped drinking and waited for the call. At some level it was all sorted out. I didn't know how and I didn't care. I started thinking of Dawn to blot out thoughts of Gail, which worked for a couple of days. Then I gave in to it.

The by-pass had snarled me up too long. Now the

dash clock was telling me I would have to press on. I chose a car in the outside lane and played at matching its pace.

Stonehouse, Dursley, Thornbury - keeping touch. The fog had lifted up, into a grey sky with a promise of rain in the West. Over there somewhere the Severn gapes into the Bristol Channel and there's a bridge that leads to Wales. I could take these last few cases and keep driving, to Cardiff, to Swansea, to Pembroke. I wonder if the ferry is running to Rosslare. There's always a market for this stuff with so many people out there trying to push the sensory envelope.

But I won't. The bridge that John is going to cross lies in the other direction; I would hate to miss an appointment. It's just not professional.

M4, M32 - the motorway roundabout. I suppose that means you do seventy around it, legally, if it didn't mean you would fly off before you could get round. Perhaps on the bike. No, not even on the bike.

I have lost control of this. It's supposed to be a job, with or without a contract. I know what John's responsibilities are. Now he's gone too far. The ground gets thinner over here. There's a danger of falling through. I look like a crazy man in the mirror. My eyes are bulging, as if there is too much pressure behind them, as if my heart is beating too fast and the blood is trying to burst out and take my eyes in the flow. I never asked for any of this. Where is it that you have to pay the price, just because you've accepted the money? Truth is, once you elect to ride a tiger, you may never dismount.

Down, past the looming bulk of the Dower House, possessively overlooking the elevated section of the 32, feeling like a long time since I'd been in a city – so many people.

I sat in traffic rubbing my face, trying to forget the hunger. Then I missed the turn for the A420, like an idiot, and had to backtrack. I was supposed to know what I was doing.

I found the right road, made my way up to the shop and parked on the single yellow outside.

I had never been entirely sure what line of business they were in. The proprietor's name, sign-written above the shop-front, gave no clue. There were a few, peculiarly shaped machine parts in the window and, inside, an old fashioned pin board behind the counter, displaying sets of replacement dial gauges. I took the cases, placed them on the counter and waited.

It was five or ten minutes before anyone came out, an insouciant looking youth I hadn't seen before.

'Sign for these,' I said, 'and hurry up, will you, I'm running late.'

There was a delivery note. God knows why they wanted one. Perhaps it made the consignment appear legitimate. If any auditors bothered to check, though, they would only find that the details on the note were made up. He scrawled a name and I gave him the top copy. I guessed he didn't know what was in the boxes. Perhaps no one on here knew and it was just a way of keeping the real customer at one remove. I checked the time and removed myself.

Every fucker in the world pulled out in front of me as I headed out on the 420. Kingswood was heaving. What day was it? Christmas shopping? I wouldn't be doing any of that.

A bike shot past me at about fifty, tarring the rest of we two-wheelers with the same brush. I wanted to catch him up and tip him off his bike, to teach him a lesson. I was tired and hungry and pissed off and hungry and tired. A van pulled out and forced me to brake. *Fuck, fuck, fuck.*

I should have gone back to the M32. Too built up. Too many traffic lights. This is the last trip and it's supposed to go according to plan. One more drop to go.

BARBURY

A46 going north, stuck behind a caravan doing forty. *Who the fuck takes a caravan out in December?*

I listened to the radio for a while to take my mind off the dwindling time. The song talked about searching for a face in every place. Where's *Road to Hell* when you need it? Then, of course, straight afterwards came Gail's traffic report.

"It's been a difficult day on the road for many people, with dense fog in western parts of the country and a number of accidents as a consequence, including a major accident on the westbound M50 into Wales at Junction 3. Police are advising that it will probably take them the rest of the afternoon to clear that one up and that motorists should be aware that the westbound carriageway is down to one lane. Travellers eastbound can also expect delays, as drivers there are insisting on slowing down to look at the accident. Alternative routes are recommended, if at all possible.

In Cheshire the M6 is almost at a standstill between junctions 17 and 19 and this seems to be down to combination of bad visibility and sheer weight of traffic. As we move further towards rush hour we can probably expect conditions to deteriorate there.

It's all motorways this time. The M18 is experiencing slow-moving traffic around the A1 junction as a result of road works in both directions, with a contra-flow operating there and the M4 coming in towards London is currently chock-a-block with traffic, following the accident earlier near to the slip-road of the A355 to Slough at Junction 6. That's it for now – I'll be back for my next bulletin in around half an hour."

Thank you, Gail. The M4 thing won't affect me until later, but it's always nice to know in advance.

I checked the time and turned off the radio. Time for quiet.

Perhaps I could talk to Dave. John is no threat. He exists only to do his job and try and have a little fun. What's the problem? He's a loyal employee. But then, it's not about logic and reason, it's about visceral forces that spew forth, however hard you try to hold them down. John is my responsibility; if anyone were going to tidy him up it should have been me – I'm a tidy person.

The caravan had slowed to thirty specifically to piss me off, exactly as an impenetrable stream of traffic decided to come the other way.

I hate crawling along the open road; the journey is no longer a flight of the imagination. The unreality of it is caught up in the momentum – you are travelling in a hyperspace just outside, but consequent upon, the environment in which you are travelling. If you go too slowly, the environment catches up with you and you're just another part of it. It's not that you can ignore the exigencies of the road as you travel, simply that you can feel yourself apart, rather than a part.

The caravan went all the way to the M4, trailing me with it, like an additional load. He must have been able to see the queue building up behind him, yet he had ignored every opportunity to pull over and let us past.

M4 roundabout, shaking my fist out of the window, like an idiot, as if that made any difference. He won't even know what the problem's been. The last few cases slip round on the floor as I speed on to the slip road.

From here on in the junctions count down to the inevitable conclusion. To start with they will be many miles apart; at the end they will come closer and closer together. It will be like hurtling towards earth under the force of gravity, all the time accelerating to a stop.

That's the process, though you could say that the process started three days ago. Then, you could say that the process started the moment I accepted a drink off Dave in that dingy pub. You could say it started the day I left college, all those years ago, almost on the flip of a coin. Where do you find the beginning of a process? Does a process have a beginning or does it somehow crystallise out of a myriad small choices that you have made, none of which seemed significant at the time?

I hate documentaries about the late and great. They can be fascinating enough, in their way, but all the time they're telling you how the subject overcame their early hardships to forge their first, transcendent successes you already know how it's all going to end. Sometimes the end defines the life: James Dean smashed up in his Porsche Spyder; Saki saying 'Put that bloody cigarette out...' on a battlefield in France in 1916; Newton an old man and reputedly still a virgin; others from overdoses and stupid misjudgements that could have been avoided if someone had just been able to say to them, 'If you do this or that tomorrow you'll be dead, for dead certain.'

Who knows when they are going to die? Only suicides or those executed by the state or by military authorities. If you knew when you were going to die would you behave any differently? I bet some would go on - 'That's A1 smack. The guy told me it was the best. Nothing can go wrong.' So off they go and choke on their own vomit at three o'clock in the morning with no one around to save them, because no one could be bothered to stick around any longer listening to their self-satisfied bullshit.

When is John going to die? Somewhere between four and five o'clock this afternoon, I would say. I don't think Terence is likely to hang about. It would be helpful if he'd found a better implement than that evil looking screwdriver, but at least he's had the benefit of practice. Why don't I mind?

So hungry, so empty.

Leigh Delamere, Chippenham, Lyneham, Wootton Bassett. Swindon.

I turned off at Junction 15 and headed south towards Marlborough. One mile, then right towards Wroughton on the B4005. It's going back on yourself, but it saves time in the end. Left at the corner, along the straight, narrow road and up the ridge. Right into the car park for the castle. There they were.

In this job it's always twos. I only know these two by the colour of their hair: one is fair and one is dark, like Starsky and Hutch. The dark one is the driver; the other one watches. They have a Lotus Carlton painted a bile yellow. Sacrilege.

I pulled up opposite and got out, went straight round the back and started to unload. The dark one came over.

'You're late.'

'And?'

'You're fucking late. Two o'clock. That's the arrangement. Guess what the fucking time is.'

'No, I give up, you tell me.'

'You're smart, you're really fucking smart. We got better things to do that sit up here for an hour while you wank yourself off in some lay-by.'

'I'm here. Here's the stuff. Take it. Piss off.'

He looked back towards the fair one, sitting on the bonnet of the Carlton, 'Oi Phil, he's giving me lip.'

I had the three cases out by now, stacked up by my front bumper. He was standing a few paces off, with his stupid fucking face and his gelled-up hair. He looked like the sort of shit you would hate at any age. I'd always thought that. I'd always hated the drop. I particularly didn't want to have to put up with him on this windy, overcast day when there was important stuff coming up.

'These are yours,' I said. 'You want them, shit-head?' I stood by the cases and dared him to pick them up.

He was on me. He didn't try to punch, or anything like that, he simply launched himself in my direction with his hands stretched out. I twisted away, but he caught me and we both went down.

The tarmac was cold and I didn't want to be on it. I pushed him to the side and attempted to get out from under, but it just helped him get a hand free. He punched me twice in the face. The second time my head bounced on the ground. Three would be too much. I pushed him over further and wrestled my hand up to his throat. I pressed my fingers into his Adam's apple. I tried to rip at his windpipe. That hurt. Then I had him over. He got to his feet quickly and got in a kick. I rolled, but he still caught me in the back. That hurt me. I rolled again, out of range.

Now we were both on our feet. He came at me the same way as before, like the stupid cunt he was, no doubt expecting me to fall away again. Cunts like that can't adapt to the unexpected. I stepped right inside him, cut the distance between us and put the lot behind my right fist, full force into the bridge of his nose. The gristle cracked under my knuckles and his knees went.

He just managed to stop himself going down, which was good, because I was just thinking about stamping on his throat and seeing what came of it.

Now the fair one had come up and I was getting ready for phase two, but he grabbed hold of his mate and pulled him back.

'Leave it,' he said.

'I think he's broke my nose.'

'Leave it. He's shit. He's not worth it. Look at him. He's shit.'

I stood my ground. The fair one picked up two of the cases and started to back off, 'Get the other box.'

Dark looked at me and spit out the blood that had run into his mouth. Some of it caught me in the face. I still didn't move. He picked up the case and backed over to his car. The blood on his face formed a red beard.

He drove straight at me when they left, but I wasn't going to move. They didn't have the bottle. That and they were right: I was shit – I wasn't worth it.

BARBURY CASTLE

It was getting late. Terence would be waiting. I stood for a while, until I felt the cold, then reached into the van for my jacket.

I'm not quite ready. Not quite. It's all still a little mixed up. I'd like to feel I had it sorted out. In all the times I've dropped at the car park I've never actually visited the castle. So let's give John a moment to himself. We can call it 'John's time'. What's an hour between friends?

I walked through the car park and the muddy field that led to the castle. The castle is misnamed – it's really an iron-age hill fort. To the north Swindon is laid out on the plain. Wroughton is to the left, Lydiard Tregoze in the space beyond. To the south the ridge rolls away to Avebury and Silbury Hill, towards the white horses and Wansdyke.

There was no one else about. Most people would be at work, like myself, or have better things to do then freeze themselves rigid on a windy hillside. I passed a stark copse of trees, where a parliament of rooks announced my coming, debating the issues of the day in their cracked voices. My last company, it seems, is to be a gaggle of rooks in the treetops. Or is it a 'murder' of crows? Everything is symbolic if you look hard enough.

I reached the eastern entrance. The castle was a field encircled by two banks separated by a ditch. I ascended the inner bank to my left and started to walk clockwise; that would seem to be the right direction. The inner rampart was much higher than I had anticipated, the ditch between that and the outer much deeper. The difference must have been even greater in antiquity. My head was beginning to hurt where it had impacted with the tarmac; the wind was too cold for my thin jacket.

I wonder what Dawn would have been like in a different context. All this time she's more or less just constituted an overnight stop on the delivery route. I've been telling her for months that she needs to get away. I've never even heard her tell me she's been on holiday anywhere, except for two mud-drenched days at a festival somewhere in the Midlands, along with the other John and his low-life cronies.

Now I'm wondering who the advice was for. I've been travelling. I've done a hell of a lot of travelling, but I've never been away. By the time I got to thinking that there might be some way out, it was all too late. Yet it must surely have been possible, early on in this process, to have done something about it. I could have left the country for a month and seen what I could find. I've never travelled by boat, except for ferries across the Channel. I've never been on a plane further than southern Spain.

You should only give advice that you'd be prepared to

take yourself. I could have collected Dawn from work and surprised her with some flight tickets. An evening's notice would be all she'd need to pack and prepare. She could have told her boss at the pet-food hypermarket to fuck off and then fucked off with me to wherever the sun shone and you could eat for peanuts. I wonder whether her prison pallor would manage to survive in those circumstances. We could have tried and just seen what happened, even if, in the final analysis, we were some kind of mismatch. Does that really matter? Only, no one likes to be lied to and I would have to turn up at the airport with a passport in the name of someone called Ben. So, instead, it's goodbye Dawn and it looks like we'll never know.

One day, when she'd had too much to drink, she said to me, 'You road people have got no staying power,' and I laughed at her and said, 'Where the hell did that come from?' I carried on drinking my beer and shaking my head at her expense, but in the morning I was trying to get what she was getting at *in vino veritas*. Now I think I have an idea. Yet I'm staying the course right up to the edge of my fate, and beyond, because somehow that's my solution.

I had reached the western entrance to the castle. The wind was cutting through my jacket. Down the slope to my left there was something like a horseracing course. To the right a dished barrow, just beneath the ramparts. Between that and myself an information plaque

I climbed up the embankment and recommenced my

circuit. Behind me the hills faded into the distance. Ahead they continued, the next earthwork silhouetted against the sky a mile or two away. The Ridgeway, the oldest road in Britain. It dates back into prehistory, links together many remarkable landmarks. From here I could walk to Datchet, almost the entire way to the unit. That would be a way to travel – no jams, no impenetrable clouds of spray off the wagons, travelling with a different sort of wagon, going at a pace that suits the natural rhythms, close to the spreading sky. You could take account of the scenery laid out below, rather than having to concentrate on the visible road ahead. A journey like that would credit a celebratory arrival. And how long it would take.

I am back where I started. John's journey is almost done. It's fitting that this place has tombs for the dead. And the Ridgeway. It reminds me of happier times. It reminds me that I have an appointment to keep. I would have liked to have spoken to someone, one last time, but if not, then this was the place to be alone. The rooks are telling me that the wind is cold, but that after the cold is spring. I wish them luck.

COMING BACK

My tired old Cavalier trundled away from familiar roads. The finite field that we had occupied together was left behind.

Gail sat in my passenger seat, quiet. I could feel her watching me at work behind the wheel, satisfied that I had everything under control and she could sit back and enjoy the ride. She was dressed lightly in a cotton skirt patterned with a new-age design, a T-shirt with a V-neck and her green denim jacket. Her green eyes looked towards the scenery coming up ahead of the car. Her hand lay on the seat next to her and I wanted to fold it in mine, but you can't do that sort of thing when you're driving.

The land rolled out, from closed field to open grassland, chalk down with lush stands of trees. The sun teased through gaps in the cloud, rays of light, patchwork upon patchwork. We rode through it, sometimes in shade, sometimes in light, always within the ferment of spring.

'Where are we gong?' she said.

'Wayland's Smithy.'

I could see her searching her memory for a reference, 'And what would that be?'

'It's a tumulus.'

'Oh yes?'

'A chambered burial mound. It's supposed to be special, unique sort of thing.'

That seems to be enough. She's in the spirit of the outing.

I move between the patches of light, warm in the car. It's quiet: the kids aren't out from school yet. Time is fluid. The space we inhabit is set apart from normal rules. Gail has made magic with the physics. Now she's reading the map for me, as if a map could apply in such unreal conditions.

Up through Lambourn, the B4000, following the curves of the bluff hills, past the cupola of Ashdown House and across the top to Ashbury, then down, eastwards on the B4507, looking for the right turning, climbing back up the ridge to the car park.

There is only one other car and that doesn't seem to have any occupants. Gail is quiet, looking at the map.

'Wayland's Smithy,' she says.

We rise from the car park to the broad, open grasslands undulating into the distance. The clouds cast their shadows onto the landscape and I hold her hand until she smiles. We walk together, with the grass brushing against our shoes. Each step takes us further from the selves we've had to put up with to get our coursework done. The pure self comes out in the open air.

The sign directs us towards the barrow; a lark rises

from the hedgerow as we pass onto the farm track, exactly as it's scripted to do. I try to think of ways to maintain the supposed ironic consideration of the trip, but ironies don't seem to work here.

From the farm track we turn and head down the Ridgeway, between mature hedgerows and fields of corn. One or two small spots of rain catch my face and I look up into the sky. I stumble on a furrow in the track and Gail puts out a hand to steady me. After the car journey our progress feels slow. It takes time to adapt to new expectations. Gail has somehow manipulated time. It works in a different way.

'How far is it supposed to be, Ben?' she says.

I can't answer that. I may have been here before, a long time ago, but I can't be sure. It's the feel that's familiar, as if I'm suddenly connected to some ancient truth.

In fact it's further than I thought it would be, judging from the map in the car park. We've set off on some major expedition. It continues to be too far right up until the point where we arrive. I lead her through the gate and in amongst the trees. She walks on, to where the four stones stand at the opening of the mound. She gazes into the mouth of the tomb and it gazes back. I catch her up and place my hand, for a moment, on the small of her back. There are raindrops soaked into her T-shirt, unnoticed except by me.

'What's the smithy bit?'

'Wayland was the Saxon god of metalworking.

When the Saxons came this tomb had already been here for thousands of years. They had no idea what sort of people would construct something so huge so they ascribed it to one of their deities. Legend has it that if you left your horse and a silver coin here overnight Wayland the Smith would have shoed your horse by the morning.'

'How do you know all these things, Ben?'

'I'd love to tell you it's years of erudition organised into an encyclopaedic array of knowledge, but I have to admit that I read it on the information board over there.'

The sunlight has caught her through the trees. So far we haven't seen another soul. We go together into the cross of the tomb. Someone has left flowers – wildflowers, I think. Then we are on top of the mound, walking towards the tail of the tumulus. I imagine some huge creature concealed beneath the surface. We are walking on its back. It rests out these millennia, waiting for civilisation to crumble before it can wake and rise again, when men no longer fly or sail or drive, when the world is as far as you can walk and time is measured out in steps, when Gail and I walk again alone through the grass.

We return to the gate and I say 'Look' and bend down and pick up a stone.

'Look at this,' I say.

'It's just a stone.'

It's a smooth stone, shaped like the butt of a cigar. There's a perfectly round hole in one end that disappears into the stone, but doesn't come out the other end, like it used to fit once onto the end of a rod. I try to tell her that it's an important find, that I've never seen anything like it before in all my born days and she retorts that it looks like nothing more than a fossilised pencil rubber and that it's just some minor geological anomaly. I put it in her hand and tell her that she should keep it: you should always keep your good luck close at hand.

Then we return the same way, but cross the farm track instead of turning down it, up towards the hill of the white horse.

I want to see the hill fort, but she has a hankering to continue to the brow of the hill. We separate and our paths diverge. I look back for her, but she's already striding out for the horizon. I cross the ditch and climb the dyke and select a direction to walk around the perimeter of the fort, whichever feels right. Nothing feels right without her.

I've walked anti-clockwise and I've had a fine view of the plain. I can't see Gail anywhere. I pace down, towards the white horse. I can't believe there are no more people here. I am on my own. Everything is quiet – not even the distant sound of traffic. I sit down by the horse's head and fold my arms around my legs. I close my eyes and try to hear every sound, from the flutter of wing-beats to the worms in the ground. Time doesn't matter. My time is nothing compared to the incomprehensible spans afforded to the hills and valleys, just a moment crawling along the ground, standing, pushing my head towards the sky. All I can manage is a few short journeys before I'm forced to come to a permanent rest. One's time is comprised of journeys of every kind, some more important than others.

I open my eyes. I must have been here for half an hour without noticing. I have a sudden thought and stand up. She is nowhere. I cast my eyes up, towards the castle, across the arc of the white horse, into the valley. I look back towards the hill and I see her striding down towards me. She's strong and straight and she looks as if she could walk forever. Her skin looks tanned in the sunlight. She looks like she belongs here. Why, so often, do I feel so out of place? All I can do is watch her.

'Wotcha,' she says.

'Hi.'

'This is the White Horse then.'

'Yes, the Uffington White Horse.'

'Some people say it's actually a dragon. That mound down there is Dragon Hill, where St George slew the beast. Where its blood spilled no grass has ever grown.'

'Er...?' I go to ask her, but before I can she says, 'I read in on the information board in the car park before we set out.'

I can't bring myself to kiss her, because it's suddenly all too much. She's far too perfect to come close to. I stand there. She reaches out and takes hold of my hand.

'Come on,' she says, 'let's go and have a look.'

We meander back slowly in the darkness. We eat well at

a pub. I have just enough money to cover it. There's only a few miles to go and I don't need directions. The plan has gone tremendously well. I've fooled her into thinking it was all a kind of joke and she's gone along with it and made it work. I think she enjoyed it. She always looks natural, whatever she does. She's smiling now, so it's a good time to ask her.

'So, what are your plans after we graduate?'

'I've been thinking of that. There's a chance of me doing some work at the school where I've been doing my teaching practice.'

'You like it there, don't you?'

'It's not too bad. There are worse places. I thought it might be worth a shot. It might mean I can make a hole in my debt mountain.'

'I know what you mean. I need to do something about that myself.'

'So what are you going to do?'

'Me? Well I might take a few weeks off and then get some casual work to get some money together. I don't have any career plans as yet. I want to get through my exams first. One thing I do know though.'

'What?'

'I'm not going to be too far away from you.'

'Ben, you're a romantic fool.'

'Isn't that what this day's all about?'

It may have been part of the game, but I knew that she was pleased that we would be staying together. That was why she was going to jump at the possibility of staying at a local school until she could get things sorted.

'Casual work's fine for the short term, but what about the long term? Any idea what you might do?' She sounded like she cared.

'Well, I'm not sure yet, and I don't know why, but I've always thought that I'd end up doing something really good.'

Time rolled on and time laid its tracks as lines behind us on the tarmac, connecting the past unbreakably to the ever-passing moment, the two of us together in the car.

Hungerford, Thatcham, Newbury, radio turned off – motorway running smoothly – no sign of the delays Gail mentioned earlier. All well and good – should hit the unit before the worst of the rush hour. Not that the rush is ever confined to any hour; around the western interchanges you can get clogged up on a Sunday – perhaps even worse on a Sunday, there are so many more amateurs about.

I rubbed the graze on the back of my head. It hurt like pain. I rubbed a piece of grit out and it hurt less. How the road gets into your head.

The traffic streamed along with me, as if we had a common purpose. I could see us all, heading into the unit, queuing up in an orderly fashion to face the ministrations of Terence.

Now that it's almost complete, I can see how incomplete I've left it. Dawn is going to wait. She's going to keep on waiting. Maybe John should have left a note. He doesn't really have that facility of care but, if he lied his way in, he should surely have been able to lie his way out. Leaving it open-ended was like failing to finish a job. A job has to be finished. If not, what can you say about yourself? John: 'He did a half-arsed job, then he couldn't be bothered.' Ben: 'Thought a good job, then passed when it came to actually seeing it through.'

I don't think it's going to affect her long-term, but I've piped up so many times about the shortcomings of the other John and, now, my John has gone and compounded the list of disappointments. Then, that seems to be how I am these days. This is how John has it. His eyes were open all the way along, even if he wasn't paying proper attention.

The AA were attending to someone on the hard shoulder. Perhaps it was something to do with the earlier delays. The car was a nearly new Lexus – the owner wouldn't like that, though it could equally be the case that he'd called out rescue to fix a blockage in his favourite meerschaum – people do that sort of thing. Either way, you wouldn't find me hanging about on the hard shoulder. It demonstrates too much trust in the discipline of the traffic in the nearside lane. I once saw a wagon stray onto the shoulder and wipe out an old Citrôen sitting there with its bonnet up. The guy performed a high jump of Olympic standard trying to avoid the remains of his car, hurtling towards him, backed by tons and tons of irresistible momentum. You have to sit up the embankment and wait, out of harm's way, even if it's pissing down, which it's about to do any minute now.

The rain came as drizzle and came back churned up as spray. Those of us with any sense slowed down to reduce the risk.

The trouble with filing away our histories in simplified form is, that while you might think it's the central kernel of an experience that merits preservation, sometimes the truth is in the apparently insignificant details. Later, these details might take on a significance all of themselves and give lie to what you thought was the truth. You get fooled because the truth you've distilled out is pure and clear in the glass. It leaves a strong taste.

I went up to college to look at the degree results posted on the notice board outside the S.U. I breathed a sigh of relief when I saw that I'd passed okay. So far so good. I knew Gail had passed. I couldn't have expected otherwise. I celebrated with more than one drink in the bar. Some of my drinking buddies were in there, so the thing turned into a bit of an afternoon session. Still, I was so elated that everything had gone well, and that I was released from all that pressure that, I found myself unable to get drunk, only happy. In the late afternoon I hitched a lift into town and walked lightly over to Bridget's house, to see what Gail was doing. She was packing.

'What are you up to?' I said.

'Ben, I've been trying to get in touch with you, I have

to leave today.'

'What?'

'I've got a job.'

'At the school.'

'No, in East Anglia.'

'Another school?'

'No, my uncle's found me a job as a researcher for a radio station. I told you he worked in the media, didn't I? Anyway, someone's let them down, so they need someone to replace them right away. It's a tremendous opportunity.'

'But our plans...'

'Change of plans. It doesn't matter. You can follow me to East Anglia when you find some way to get yourself set up.'

'I don't know anything about East Anglia.'

She carried on putting her things in her case: the black leggings; the green denim jacket.

'You can't go. Can't you put it off?'

'Ben, come on. The starting salary's great compared to what I'd get teaching and it's a real opportunity. I've already said yes and I can't let Uncle Charles down. It just means that you have to come with me over there when you can sort it out.'

Some kind of wheel or cog set into motion in my chest. I could feel it physically. It wasn't a thing I had felt before. I looked down at the ground and then I looked at her for a moment and did the strangest thing. I didn't say another word to her. I closed my mouth so that no words could come out and then I turned around and I walked out of the house. I went back to my shitdump shared house. I don't know whether she tried to call or whether she sent any letters, because I was gone. I went straight back home and started looking for a job. Against my expectations it took no time. Within days I was inputting sales data into a terminal in a different town and my college life seemed like a brief dream of daylight before a return to the darkness of the winter night. College-Ben ceased to be and a previous working-Ben manifestation reappeared in familiar guise, ony now better qualified and even more out of place.

I've never been able to work out why I walked out of the door with such sudden determination. I used to think it was because I thought she'd thrown my love back in my face, that I should have been taken into consideration in her decision making. I used to think that perhaps my inflated ego couldn't take the affront when things had been going so well. Now I'm not so sure. I think that some aspect of escaping from myself is in my nature, that now that things were going to become a bit settled after all that unfulfilled promise, with everything to play for, I couldn't bring myself to become something that was solid and easily defined. Maybe I was envious that she was going to be somebody while I was going to remain a nobody. I headed for the door without looking back. Unfortunately, now, I have to look back and, when I do, I see that I left a situation that was unresolved, like an unfinished job. I hate an unfinished job: I don't stop driving until the deliveries are done.

Sometimes I get the wrong end of the stick. The dark-haired guy isn't a potential suitor of Gail's, he's just some media guy that she knows. He probably works for Human Resources and he's in the early stages of grooming her for television, the next rung on her career ladder. They've been hinting about her leaving on the radio for weeks. She'd look right on TV.

But how could I ever approach her again?

'Ben, what a surprise, how did you know where I lived?'

'Well, I followed you home once. In fact I've followed you round a lot and watched you in all your private moments. I used to spend lots of time sitting on the wall at the bottom of your garden and once I actually got inside your house and had a look around your things. I got into your life without an invitation, without your knowledge and rooted around for my own, selfish satisfaction. I'm guilty of the worst sort of violation of your personal space. I'm actually a bit of a criminal and my actions have probably put you in some danger. Shall we go out for a drink and reminisce about how I once walked out of your life without the courtesy of offering any reasons or, indeed, that I didn't have any worthwhile reasons and that I never spoke to you again, even though I know that you loved me and it would have been the simplest thing in the world to have come over to East Anglia with you and done something worthwhile with my existence. Yes, I could have signed up for an MA or done anything. I didn't have anything special to do or anywhere special to be, except that I did have somewhere special to be, which was right next to you, but in actual fact I'm a bit of a fucking head-case when it comes to things like that and I can't recognise a good thing when I see it. And, if I do see it, I'll probably have a bit of a funny turn and drive as far away from it as I can possibly get.'

Reading, Wokingham, Bracknell – the drizzle now bordering on sleet. I could have turned off at Junction 14 and found the road to Lambourn. I could have followed the road up to the Ridgeway and walked up White Horse Hill and looked for memories. It's too late now. But what would I have found anyway? A windswept, lonely place, with cold rain slanting onto the heath. You can never go back. Time flows downhill to the sea.

Now I want it over and done with. The road's getting busier and it's getting harder to see. Down to forty. I want it over.

I know what's been happening now: Ben is driving John is driving the van. Whatever the reasons for that are, they were in place a long time ago. I've been struggling to re-assemble myself for the entire trip and all the time I was never apart. I'm the result of my choices and whatever sundry events took place along the way. Perhaps I shouldn't be too hard on myself – a lot of it's been genuinely beyond my control. Not that that excuses the way I've reacted to what was handed to me.

I know that I would make different choices if I had the opportunity to make them again. I've decided that it's valid to regret, but I also know that you only have a whole take on a trip when it's complete. For life, you're not issued with a comprehensive set of maps. If you're the driver, then it's you who makes the choices. I hate to be a passenger.

This new century leaves me cold. It was always, 'This is what it will be like in the year 2000.' They promised us individual rocket cars and meals in a pill. Yet here I am in a white Astra van, broadly recognisable to a driver from forty years ago. It was always, 'These will be the technical advances we can expect by 2001.' They never said what was to come after. They never said what we were supposed to think, looking into the featureless future. All ideas of the future become history.

For a long time, my future has extended only as far as the end of the next trip. It's an easy step to see it finishing at the end of this last trip.

What will be left of me when I'm gone? I've failed to reproduce myself, so there's nothing there. So, what have I got? A set of furniture enough to fill a flat, cooking and dining equipment, apparatus for home entertainment, printed and recorded media, a paltry collection of adornments for wall and shelf, machines and applications for the beautification of the self, clothes and bed linen, photographs enough to fill a shoebox, memories.

Who will remember me? Dawn? She'll remember

John and how he failed to come back. After a while even that won't carry any weight.

Will, Joanna, Little Will? Little Will will hardly care. I turned up once or twice and performed the anarchic uncle act. Then I went away again and failed to write, even failed to remember your birthday. I imparted nothing of my hard-earned wit and wisdom.

Joanna? Well, she married Will, not me. I kind of came as part of the package. There was none of that smooth crossover like handing on the keys to a much-loved car. With Will she got his history with me, whether she wanted it or not. There's too much hard mileage travelling with me. I have to turn up at all of life's important stations – weddings, anniversaries and Christenings – and hang about committing faux pas with regard to the decorating. I had to turn up, one time, when you were busy sorting out the future and insist that Will take me for a prolonged thrash in the new company car. I turned up another time, when you were arguing, and forced you to thaw when you'd been planning a lengthy frost. Mostly, I suppose, I forced you to take into account someone you would never have chosen as a friend, worse still, a mirror for all your partner's worst characteristics.

That leaves Will. Since we've been grown-up boys I've felt like the pest that follows you around, bothering you with my aspirations and opinions when you were simply getting on with it. You were proud of your little brother when you were little yourself. How were you to know that I would live to disappoint you for the rest of my life? Were you pleased to have someone to show the tricks to? Did you pave the way for me at school or did you hate the fact that I stayed behind with Mum, warm in the pushchair when we saw you off?

I've bothered you emotionally and financially, when you had your own stuff to think about. I've come back and done it again. You'll remember me for drinking too much that Christmas, using your family home as a hotel, making Little Will sick on the settee by feeding him too much chocolate, making you suffer on your stag night, criticising your girlfriend before I knew she was going to be your wife, always insisting that I was right, failing to apologise about bleeding on your homework after a stupid fight. You are given, heart and soul, to Joanna and you're better off without me.

Then there are photographs – a few moments here and there from a pointless life - images of some road bruises for an accident claim, dressed up in an academic gown, holding a roll of paper that isn't even my degree. I can see it now, standing on a desk at the back of a barn across the Scottish Border, out of context, out of time, out of mind.

Now I have to think about the purgatory of that dark hall, the sum of all those outstripped lives, sitting in the twilight, with all that's precious sold off for profit.

The end of the journey is the place to ask oneself how it went. Dave used to ask me if everything had gone okay. I can see that I've dropped the right number of cases in the right places. I can see that I got them there more or less on time. Close enough, anyway, for the customer to be able to get them. The van still has a little fuel. With each moment the fuel gets lower and I get closer to home.

Maidenhead, Windsor, Slough – I could listen out for Gail on the radio one last time, but I don't think I can stand it. I need to leave it all behind on the road. I've been thinking too much and I want it to stop. There has been nothing but thought and roads, the inside of the van and the inside of my head. I long for dialogue. Instead there is the stony echo of my own small voice, calling to no one, calling out into a void of which I am the centre. No one said anything about it being like this. No one said how formless it all is at the end of things. Finally, you call out and there's no reply. From here on it's all down hill. At one time life sparked and I looked forward to how things might turn out. In those days it was all left to do. But those days are gone. Whatever there was is done and none of it has anything to do with what I thought might have been. I'm waiting for the darkness as the tree trunk finally zips shut with me inside. I go to rest at Caesar's Camp.

I like those roads that are named after their destination but then, as I've found, it's the idea of that destination that has the power and not perhaps the actual destination itself. Gail is a destination. She used to be real, but that was a long time ago. Now she's a kind of myth I've made up for myself. In Gail I see another possible self, one in which I did a better job of things and didn't end up didn't end up disappointing myself, a proper road with no suspect packages and no stalkers jabbed onto the ends of screwdrivers for the amusement of madmen. Instead I have this and there's no going back. You can't reverse down the thousands of miles of road and set out again in a different direction. But now it doesn't matter, because it's all going to stop and, finally, now that it's all come back, I can put her out of my mind.

Junction 4A – I'm back inside the M25. The one photograph I had is gone. I burnt it before I started out on this trip. I didn't like the thought of Terence or Dave getting hold of it when they were going through my things. I expunged my flat of everything that had to do with Ben or anyone he'd known or anyone to whom he was related. It didn't take very long. I packed it up and sent it all on a slow delivery to Will. All that was left was John's and he hardly left any trace. I thought I might post the photograph through Gail's letterbox, just for the mystery of it, but sometimes two ideas can't occupy the same space, so I looked at it one more time to see if I could divine its message and then burnt it and scattered the ashes.

Junction 4 – this is where I get off. I'm almost gone now. My hands are shaking on the wheel. For the first time this entire trip I've just misjudged the clutch and crunched a gear. Oddly, I don't feel hungry anymore. I'm slowed to a crawl and reality has caught up.

A few more turns to the industrial park and there's the

unit. The end of the road – all I have to do is park up and my journey is complete.

HOME

I don't know whether it's the rain, but it's darker inside than I remember. It's also quieter. All I can hear are the raindrops pattering on the corrugated roof far above.

I have left the seat of the van for the last time. The engine is ticking with the raindrops as it goes cold.

I loiter outside the big shutter door. It is half-closed. Have they had a delivery or are they waiting for me to deliver myself?

I can't hear them inside. Stranger still, I can't hear the sound of the video. Yet they must be inside because their cars are parked by the wall.

I stay at the door, looking into the quiet shade. Nothing is moving. I think of the knight-errant at the mouth of the cave, ready to face the fate beast, and I try to see myself from the outside. I can't. There is no music, no fancy camera work, no glorious Technicolor on this drab day.

I feel stupid, because I'm going to stop putting off going in because I'm getting damp, and not for any of the other reasons. So in I go.

It is still and dark, like a stage before the lights come up. The walls are alive with the hum of activity. I walk through thick time, in which each second pours like syrup.

My hands belong to someone else. I hold them up and look at them, a distant hand sculpture encased in glass. I move slowly; each moment devours my motive power.

Why can't they show themselves? Anything would be better than this game. Why can't they turn on the lights? They want me to find them. They expect me to come in like any other day and hand back the keys to Dave and tell them how the trip went and whether there were any problems on the way.

In Dave's office, everything is in place, except Dave. I walk into Terence's room. Here the same. I check meticulously to make sure.

The hum is louder. The whole world consists of this building, in here with me, now. The whole world fizzes with potential.

I feel like you do when you are about to cry, but cannot bring yourself to tears. How can all those journeys simply stop here, in a world of eight thousand square feet? How can all that fade, with me?

I go back to the loading area, amongst the stacks of boxes and packing crates. I should turn on the light and finish the game, but part of me doesn't want to break the rules.

I am at the end of myself. Desperation is not how I imagined. Where I expected the pure clarity of the moment, there is just distance. Everything is viewed down the wrong end of a telescope and the head's adrift in a sea of incomprehension. I now know why people say that it felt like the accident happened to someone else.

I breathe sharply and blink, because my eyes are dry. The stacks of boxes are stalagmites in a cavern. I am underground.

Please come and stop this. I want it to stop.

Think of the moment. Stay right here, in the moment. There is no 'was' and no 'to come'.

Every breath is sharp, because I have forgotten how to breathe. In the present, all things have to be relearned.

I am moving so slowly now. They must be watching me, knowing that I am out of place, enjoying the fact that John is an idiot prey, who has driven himself up and walked right in.

Come on, then. I know what I'm doing. John wants the questions to stop. Ben wants an answer to why he has betrayed himself, and kept on betraying himself, for all these years.

I can hardly move at all. I am unsteady on my feet, like these are my first steps. I am reducing to nothing as each moment passes to the next. If it doesn't happen soon I will have set into stone.

Why don't you come out and stop this? Do Ben a favour, so he doesn't have to think anymore. He's done too much thinking, for one lifetime, and none of it has done him any good. *Come out of the dark and finish it. What are you waiting for?*

… Hello, Dave.

He looks small lying down. Whoever did this worked

comprehensively: when the shaft of the first spade broke they picked up another one. He is red turf, cut out from himself.

I look and feel embarrassed. It's like I've caught him naked, unexpectedly. My breath slows down, then stops. Terence: he could do this. I want to know. I have to know.

Terence has come to rest behind the big crate we use for storing flow-pack. He too is small without his soul, but then his head has gone. He lies in the shadow of the crate and I try to understand. Then I feel stupid, because I have to look for his head in the dark.

It takes time. I cover every corner of the building. I check even the drawers and filing cabinets. I look in the waste bin in the toilet. I dig deep into the flow-pack. It's my duty to find out. Specca's friends have been. I can see that. It's not long since they've been, but what about the head?

I'm lost. I go back to Terence, expecting him to tell me the answer. I bend down to him and he tells me. I open my mouth.

There is hair where his neck has been, pasted with crimson glue. My stomach retches, but there is nothing to expel.

His head has been beaten into the cavity of his chest. I'm looking at the top of his scalp, level with his shoulders. His eyes see inside of him, where eyes should never see. My stomach convulses one more time and I gag back the acid that reaches the back of my tongue.

In the outside the rain wets my head and soaks my shirt. Dave and Terence are stopped in the space inside. We've all reached journey's end. I had never thought what might come next. Now I have to think. The van is looking at me, but I know it stays here.

I have my back to the building, but Dave and Terence still fill my field of vision. I try to think it through, logically, as if logic has anything to say in such a situation. I can't square it with any experience, because there is nothing in there with which to compare.

Then it's odd: there's all this to see, to keep seeing. It overflows my head. It exceeds my capacity. Yet there is still this unexpected possibility of a future – a featureless landscape that I now have to map out, somehow.

All this to see, yet of all things I see most clearly: a girl in a mauve dress in a tea shop on a bright morning in a brighter spring.

Printed in Great Britain
by Amazon